The route to your roots

When they look back at their formative years, many Indians nostalgically recall the vital part Amar Chitra Katha picture books have played in their lives. It was **ACK – Amar Chitra Katha** – that first gave them a glimpse of their glorious heritage.

Since they were introduced in 1967, there are now **over 400 Amar Chitra Katha** titles to choose from. **Over 100 million copies** have been sold worldwide.

Now the Amar Chitra Katha titles are even more widely available in **1000+ bookstores all across India**. Log on to www.ack-media.com to locate a bookstore near you. If you do not have access to a bookstore, you can buy all the titles through our online store **www.amarchitrakatha.com**. We provide quick delivery anywhere in the world.

To make it easy for you to locate the titles of your choice from our treasure trove of titles, the books are now arranged in six categories.

Epics and Mythology
Best known stories from the Epics and the Puranas

Indian Classics
Enchanting tales from Indian literature

Fables and Humour
Evergreen folktales, legends and tales of wisdom and humour

Bravehearts
Stirring tales of brave men and women of India

Visionaries
Inspiring tales of thinkers, social reformers and nation builders

Contemporary Classics
The Best of Modern Indian literature

Amar Chitra Katha Pvt Ltd

© Amar Chitra Katha Pvt Ltd, 2009, Reprinted February 2017,
ISBN 978-81- 8482-258-8
Published by Amar Chitra Katha Pvt. Ltd., 201 & 202, Sumer Plaza,
2nd Floor, Marol Maroshi Road, Andheri (East), Mumbai- 400 059. India
Printed at M/s Indigo press (I) Pvt Ltd., Mumbai.
For Consumer Complaints Contact Tel : +91-22 49188881/82/83
Email: customerservice@ack-media.com

The route to your roots

CHANDRA SHEKHAR AZAD

Chandra Shekhar was only a little boy when he ran away to Bombay in search of adventure. Little did he know how much he would get involved in the country's freedom struggle. Those were the days when the non-cooperation movement had gathered immense momentum and it was in Varanasi that Chandra Shekhar first confronted British authority. After that there was no looking back. Assuming the surname 'Azad' he and his band of revolutionaries did much to awaken in the Indian people the desire for freedom. Martyred at the age of 25, Chandra Shekhar Azad has left an indelible mark on the history of Indian Independence.

Script
Shail Tiwari

Illustrations
H.S.Chavan

Editor
Anant Pai

Cover illustration by: Pratap Mulick

CHANDRA SHEKHAR AZAD

CHANDRA SHEKHAR WAS BORN IN 1906, IN BHANWRA, A VILLAGE IN ALIRAJPUR STATE, CENTRAL PROVINCES.* HE WAS A ROBUST, INTELLIGENT LAD.

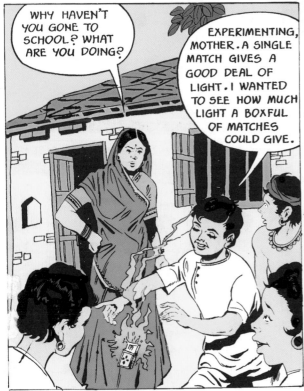

WHY HAVEN'T YOU GONE TO SCHOOL? WHAT ARE YOU DOING?

EXPERIMENTING, MOTHER. A SINGLE MATCH GIVES A GOOD DEAL OF LIGHT. I WANTED TO SEE HOW MUCH LIGHT A BOXFUL OF MATCHES COULD GIVE.

HAVEN'T I TOLD YOU THAT FIRE IS DANGEROUS?

BUT IT IS ALSO USEFUL, MOTHER. IT CHASES AWAY DARKNESS.

* NOW MADHYA PRADESH.

1

AN HOUR LATER, AS THE BOYS WERE PRACTISING ARCHERY—

WHERE DID YOU LEARN TO SHOOT SO ACCURATELY, MY SON?

FROM MY BHIL FRIENDS. WHO ARE YOU?

I TRADE IN PEARLS. I HAVE COME FROM FAR OFF BOMBAY. HAVE YOU EVER BEEN TO BOMBAY?

NO, I HAVEN'T. BUT I'D LOVE TO GO. WILL YOU TAKE ME WITH YOU WHEN YOU RETURN?

I'LL TAKE YOU TO BOMBAY, IF YOU LIKE. BUT AFTER THAT YOU ARE ON YOUR OWN.

ONE NIGHT, A FEW DAYS LATER, CHANDRA SHEKHAR QUIETLY SLIPPED OUT OF HIS HOME...

...AND SET OUT WITH THE TRADER FOR BOMBAY.

AT BOMBAY, WHEN THE TRADER WENT HIS WAY...

... CHANDRA SHEKHAR WALKED DOWN A STREET. IT LED HIM TO THE DOCKS.

WHAT AN INTERESTING PLACE BOMBAY IS! I'VE NEVER SEEN SUCH BIG SHIPS!

AS HE STOOD WONDERING WHAT HE SHOULD DO, HE SAW A PAINTER COMING TOWARDS HIM.

EXCUSE ME. CAN YOU GIVE ME A JOB?

WHY NOT! COME WITH ME.

HE WORKED FOR A FEW MONTHS. THEN—

IN WHAT WAY WILL THIS SORT OF WORK BENEFIT ME? I'LL GO TO VARANASI AND BECOME A SANSKRIT PANDIT. FATHER USED TO SAY THAT FOOD AND SHELTER ARE FREE THERE FOR STUDENTS.

THE NEXT DAY, HE BOARDED A TRAIN FOR VARANASI.

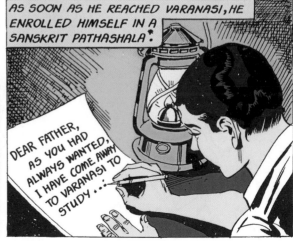

AS SOON AS HE REACHED VARANASI, HE ENROLLED HIMSELF IN A SANSKRIT PATHASHALA.*

DEAR FATHER, AS YOU HAD ALWAYS WANTED, I HAVE COME AWAY TO VARANASI TO STUDY...

* SCHOOL

IT WAS THE YEAR 1921. PEOPLE HAD RISEN IN REVOLT AGAINST THE BRITISH RULE. THE NON-CO-OPERATION MOVEMENT WAS IN FULL SWING. THERE WERE ANTI-GOVERNMENT PROCESSIONS IN VARANASI ALMOST EVERY DAY.

INQUILAB ZINDABAD!

BHARAT MATA KI JAI!

FIRED BY THEIR PATRIOTIC ZEAL, CHANDRA SHEKHAR ONE DAY JOINED A PROCESSION OF YOUNG REVOLUTIONARIES.

INQUILAB! ZINDABAD!

ARREST THE LOT. INSOLENT BRATS!

CHANDRA SHEKHAR WAS AMONG THE FIRST TO BE ARRESTED.

HE WAS PRODUCED BEFORE A MAGISTRATE.

WHAT'S YOUR NAME?

AZAD.

AFTER THAT SPEECH, THE NAME AZAD STUCK TO HIM.

CHANDRA SHEKHAR 'AZAD,' ZINDABAD!

A FEW DAYS LATER, AT ONE OF THEIR SECRET MEETINGS —

COMRADES, AN URGENT NOTICE HAS TO BE STUCK ON THE WALLS OF THE KOTWALI* WHO WILL VOLUNTEER TO DO IT?

THE KOTWALI IS HEAVILY GUARDED!

IT IS TOO RISKY A JOB.

I DON'T DARE VOLUNTEER.

WHEN NO ONE CAME FORWARD —

I'LL DO IT. I WILL GO RIGHT AWAY.

IT WAS AZAD.

* POLICE STATION

6

HE SMEARED A THICK LAYER OF GUM ON THE BACK OF THE NOTICE...

...AND A LITTLE ON ITS FACE.

THEN STICKING THE FACE OF THE NOTICE ON HIS BACK...

...HE WENT AND LEANED AGAINST A PILLAR OF THE KOTWALI.

HEY! WHAT ARE YOU DOING HERE?

LOOKING AT THE KOTWALI, SIR. I'VE JUST COME FROM MY VILLAGE TO SEE THIS CITY.

AS THE UNSUSPECTING POLICEMAN WALKED AWAY—

I'VE DONE IT!

A LITTLE LATER, THE CHIEF CAME OUT OF THE KOTWALI.

HOW DID THIS NOTICE GET HERE?

SIR, I WAS HERE ON DUTY ALL THE TIME. I CAN'T IMAGINE HOW IT COULD HAVE GOT THERE!

SUCH WAS THE DARING OF YOUNG AZAD.

TWO YEARS LATER, IN 1923, THE HINDUSTAN REPUBLICAN ASSOCIATION, A REVOLUTIONARY PARTY, ESTABLISHED A CENTRE AT VARANASI. RAMPRASAD BISMIL, ROSHAN SINGH, ASHFAQULLAH, RAJENDRA LAHIRI AND AZAD BECAME ITS STAUNCH SUPPORTERS. AT ONE OF THE PARTY MEETINGS IN 1925, AZAD CAME FORWARD WITH A QUERY.

BISMILJI, WE NEED FUNDS FOR OUR WORK. HOW ARE WE TO RAISE IT?

THERE IS ONLY ONE WAY—LET'S ROB THE RICH.

ROBBING THE RICH WILL ONLY MAKE US UNPOPULAR. LET US LOOT THE GOVERNMENT. THEN ALONE WILL THE PEOPLE SUPPORT OUR MOVEMENT.

WHAT YOU SAY IS TRUE, BISMILJI.

BUT HOW DO WE GO ABOUT IT?

BISMIL WAS READY WITH HIS PLANS FOR THE FIRST RAID.

ON THE NINTH OF AUGUST WE SEPARATELY BOARD THE B-DOWN LUCKNOW PASSENGER AT KAKORI. THEN...

EVERYTHING WENT ACCORDING TO PLAN.

WHEN THE B-DOWN LUCKNOW PASSENGER HAD TRAVELLED SOME DISTANCE FROM KAKORI —

OH, NO! I'VE LEFT MY TRUNK BEHIND AT KAKORI. HOW COULD I HAVE FORGOTTEN IT? WHAT SHALL I DO?

WHAT A CALAMITY!

ASHFAQULLAH TOOK THE CUE.

DON'T PANIC, SIR. I'LL PULL THE CHAIN AND STOP THE TRAIN.

DON'T ANY OF YOU DARE MAKE A SOUND. NO ONE WILL BE HARMED. WE ARE ONLY INTERESTED IN THE STATE TREASURY'S SAFE THAT IS ON THIS TRAIN.

MEANWHILE INSIDE THE TRAIN—

ONE STEP AND I'LL SHOOT!

HURRY! LOWER THE SAFE.

LATER—

THE GUARD AND THE DRIVER HAVE BEEN OVERPOWERED. LET'S BREAK THE SAFE, TAKE THE CASH AND GET AWAY.

AS ASHFAQULLAH BEGAN BREAKING OPEN THE SAFE—

BISMILJI, LOOK! A TRAIN!

DON'T PANIC. IT'S ONLY THE PUNJAB MAIL. LOWER YOUR ARMS AND STAND STILL.

AS THE TRAIN WHIZZED PAST, ALL OF THEM STOOD STILL.

A SECOND LATER—

QUICK! WRAP THE CASH IN SMALL BUNDLES.

BISMIL, AZAD AND THEIR FRIENDS THEN MADE THEIR WAY THROUGH THE NARROW, WINDING JUNGLE PATHS TO LUCKNOW.

THE NEXT DAY, AT LUCKNOW—

KAKORI CONSPIRACY! KAKORI CONSPIRACY!

BRITISH GOVERNMENT CHALLENGED REVOLUTIONARIES GO INTO ACTION.

LATER, WHEN EFFORTS TO TRACE THE CULPRITS WERE INTENSIFIED—

IT'S TIME FOR US TO DISPERSE, COMRADES.

ABOUT A MONTH AND A HALF LATER, EXCEPT FOR AZAD AND ONE OTHER, THE "CONSPIRATORS" WERE ROUNDED UP AND SENTENCED TO DEATH.

IT'S HIGHLY UNJUST—A DEATH SENTENCE FOR SUCH A SMALL OFFENCE!

THE BRITISH ARE MAKING A MOCKERY OF LAW AND JUSTICE. MAY THEY BE DESTROYED.

AZAD MEANWHILE HAD REACHED A HANUMAN TEMPLE AT DHIMARPUR, A SMALL VILLAGE NEAR JHANSI. ONE DAY, A PASSING VILLAGER WAS SURPRISED TO SEE A STRANGER IN THE TEMPLE.

BRAHMACHARIJI, WHERE HAVE YOU COME FROM?

I AM A WANDERING DEVOTEE OF LORD HANUMAN. I PLAN TO LIVE IN HIS TEMPLE FOR A FEW DAYS.

ONE DAY —

HEY! AREN'T YOU AZAD?

OF COURSE I AM. A DEVOTEE OF HANUMAN CAN NEVER BE ANYTHING ELSE. I MUST BE OFF.

YOU'LL HAVE TO COME TO THE POLICE STATION FIRST. THE CHIEF WANTS TO SEE YOU.

WHICH CHIEF? I HAVE ONLY ONE CHIEF— HANUMAN. GET AWAY FROM HERE BEFORE I CURSE YOU.

FRIGHTENED OUT OF HIS WITS BY AZAD'S FURY, THE POLICEMAN RAN AWAY.

THE CHIEF MUST BE MISTAKEN. HE IS A GENUINE YOGI.

WHAT A NARROW ESCAPE.

A FEW DAYS LATER, THE THAKUR OF THE VILLAGE CAME TO HIM.

BRAHMACHARIJI, WHY DON'T YOU STAY WITH ME AND TEACH AT THE VILLAGE SCHOOL. IT WILL BE CONVENIENT FOR YOU AND GOOD FOR THE CHILDREN.

AZAD ACCEPTED THE OFFER AND BEGAN TEACHING AT THE VILLAGE SCHOOL.

THE POLICE HAVE RELAXED THEIR PERSECUTION. IT'S TIME TO REORGAN-ISE THE PARTY. ONE OF THESE DAYS I MUST GO TO JHANSI.

MEANWHILE, CONTACTS WERE MADE AND AZAD'S COMRADES FROM JHANSI BEGAN JOINING HIM AT DHIMARPUR. HE BEGAN TRAINING THEM IN THE USE OF ARMS, IN THE DENSE JUNGLES OF ORCHHA.

ONE DAY, HE LEFT DHIMARPUR AND WENT TO LIVE AT JHANSI. THERE —

SIR, MY NAME IS HARI SHANKAR. I AM IN NEED OF A JOB.

BUNDELKHAND MOTOR CO.

WE HAVE VACANCIES ONLY FOR MECHANICS. YOU WILL HAVE TO LEARN THE JOB. TILL YOU DO, YOU WILL BE PAID ONLY A STIPEND.

A FEW MONTHS LATER —

YOU HAVE LEARNT BOTH DRIVING AND MOTOR — MECHANICS VERY FAST. YOU ARE NOW FIT TO DRIVE ONE OF OUR TAXIS.

FOR MONTHS HE WORKED WITH THE MOTOR COMPANY BUT NO ONE SUSPECTED THAT HARI SHANKAR WAS REALLY AZAD.

MEANWHILE, THE MOVEMENT HAD GATHERED MOMENTUM IN NORTH INDIA. SO AZAD WENT OVER TO KANPUR.

AZAD, MEET BHAGAT SINGH —FROM THE PUNJAB.

PLEASED TO MEET YOU, COMRADE. MAY MANY MORE OF US GET TOGETHER IN THE SERVICE OF THE COUNTRY.

IN SEPTEMBER 1928, THE HINDUSTAN REPUBLICAN ASSOCIATION HELD A MEETING IN DELHI.

THE PARTY'S ACTIVITIES ARE ON THE INCREASE. A DIVISION OF FUNC- TIONS IS NOW ESSENTIAL.

WE SHOULD HAVE CENTRES ALL OVER THE COUNTRY.

I SUGGEST THAT WE ADD SOCIALIST TO THE NAME OF OUR PARTY.

THUS TWO DIVISIONS WERE FORMED IN THE HINDUSTAN SOCIALIST REPUBLICAN ASSOCIATION — THE ARMY DIVISION UNDER AZAD AND THE ORGANISATION DIVISION UNDER BHAGAT SINGH.* LATER, AZAD AND BHAGAT SINGH MET AGAIN.

WE WILL ESTABLISH A SOCIETY WHICH IS FREE OF EXPLOITATION.

WE WANT FREEDOM FOR OUR COUNTRY. WE WILL NOT BEG FOR IT BUT WILL OBTAIN IT AS OUR RIGHT!

*BHAGAT SINGH HAD STOPPED SPORTING A BEARD BY THEN TO AVOID EASY DETECTION BY THE POLICE.

BY THEN, THERE WAS OPEN REBELLION AGAINST THE BRITISH GOVERNMENT. A COMMISSION WAS SENT FROM ENGLAND TO INQUIRE INTO THE GRIEVANCES OF THE PEOPLE. BUT INSTEAD OF COMING TO THE AID OF THE PEOPLE, THE "SIMON COMMISSION" AS IT WAS CALLED, TRIED TO CREATE MISTRUST AMONG THE HINDUS AND THE MUSLIMS. IT MET WITH HEAVY OPPOSITION AT LAHORE.

SIMON COMMISSION IS A HOAX!

SIMON COMMISSION, GO BACK!

WE WANT INDEPENDENCE! STOP EXPLOITING THE PEOPLE.

THE POLICE RESORTED TO A LATHI CHARGE. LALA LAJPAT RAI, A POPULAR CONGRESS LEADER, WAS FATALLY INJURED.

SEVERAL PLANS WERE MADE TO THROW BOMBS AT THE "SIMON COMMISSION" BUT NONE OF THEM WERE CARRIED OUT.

AZAD, I CANNOT BEAR IT ANY LONGER. WE MUST TAKE REVENGE.

I TOO FEEL THE SAME WAY, BHAGAT SINGH. LALAJI'S DEATH MUST BE AVENGED.

A FEW PARTY MEMBERS MET AT LAHORE AND MADE PLANS TO KILL SCOTT, THE BRITISH POLICE OFFICIAL RESPONSIBLE FOR THE DEATH OF LAJPAT RAI. AZAD, BHAGAT SINGH, RAJGURU AND JAIGOPAL WERE TO DO THE DEED.

JAIGOPAL, YOU WILL POST YOURSELF OPPO- SITE THE POLICE STATION NEAR D.A.V. COLLEGE. AS SOON AS SCOTT COMES OUT, YOU WILL SIGNAL TO BHAGAT SINGH AND RAJGURU.

AS SOON AS YOU SIGNAL TO US, WE WILL SHOOT HIM DOWN. AZAD WILL HAVE CYCLES READY FOR US TO MAKE A GETAWAY.

I WILL BE ON GUARD WITH MY MAUSER PISTOL.

ON THE APPOINTED DAY —

POLICE STATION

D.A.V. COLL

AS JAIGOPAL GAVE THE SIGNAL —

GET THEM! GET THEM!

BANG

BANG

A POLICE CONSTABLE TRIED TO NAB BHAGAT SINGH AND RAJGURU BUT AZAD APPEARED ON THE SCENE AND —

BANG

LATER, AZAD AND HIS FRIENDS MADE THEIR ESCAPE ON THE BICYCLES.

JAIGOPAL, WHO HAD MADE HIS ESCAPE BY ANOTHER ROUTE, JOINED THEM AT THEIR HIDEOUT.

WE HAVE KILLED SAUNDERS, NOT SCOTT.

NEVER MIND. SAUNDERS TOO WAS AMONG THOSE WHO CAUSED LALAJI'S DEATH.

BY THE FOLLOWING DAY, THE WHOLE OF INDIA HAD HEARD OF THE INCIDENT. POSTERS APPEARED ALL OVER LAHORE.

SAUNDERS IS DEAD! LALAJI'S MURDER HAS BEEN AVENGED!

BLOOD FOR BLOOD

HINDUSTAN SOCIALIST REPUBLICAN ASSOCIATION

FOES OF THE COUNTRY DEPART! BHARAT MATA KI JAI!

THESE REVOLUTION-ARIES WILL NOT TAKE ANYTHING LYING DOWN. NEITHER DO THEY MAKE EMPTY THREATS.

THE CHIEF OF POLICE GAVE ORDERS.

CLOSE ALL ROADS LEADING OUT OF THE TOWN.

YES, SIR!

AZAD AND BHAGAT SINGH DISCUSSED WHAT THEY SHOULD DO NEXT.

WE MUST ESCAPE FROM LAHORE.

I HAVE IT ALL PLANNED. YOU AND RAJGURU GO TO CALCUTTA...

BHAGAT SINGH, DRESSED IN BRITISH CLOTHES, ACCOMPANIED BY THE WIFE OF A REVOLUTIONARY WITH HER CHILD IN HER ARMS AND RAJGURU, DRESSED AS THEIR SERVANT, SET OUT FOR CALCUTTA.

BHABHI LOOKS A PERFECT MEM-SAHIB! WHAT SORT OF A SAHIB DO I LOOK?

FIT FOR A SERVANT LIKE ME!

MEANWHILE, AT LAHORE STATION, AZAD IN THE GUISE OF A SADHU, STOOD AT THE TICKET WINDOW, SINGING DEVOTIONAL SONGS.

MY ONLY REFUGE IS GIRIDHAR GOPAL*... NONE ELSE.... BHAIJI, A TICKET FOR MATHURA...

IN THE TRAIN—

WHERE ARE YOU GOING, MAHARAJ?

I AM A SERVANT OF GOPAL. I HAVE ONLY ONE DESTI-NATION— BRINDAVAN.

* KRISHNA.

WHEN BHAGAT SINGH REACHED CALCUTTA, HE MET HIS OLD ACQUAINTANCE— JATIN DAS, THE FAMOUS REVOLUTIONARY.

WHAT CAN I DO FOR YOU?

AZAD WANTS YOU TO COME AND HELP IN SETTING UP A BOMB FACTORY IN AGRA.

I WILL COME WITH YOU. BUT ARE ALL THE MATERIALS WE NEED AVAILABLE THERE?

YES.

LATER, AZAD TRACED BHAGAT SINGH TO AGRA WHERE WORK HAD ALREADY BEGUN.

BHAGAT SINGH! I'M GOING TO JHANSI TODAY. YOU TAKE CARE OF THINGS HERE.

THESE FREQUENT TRIPS TO JHANSI— ARE YOU PLANNING TO GET MARRIED?

I AM ALREADY MARRIED — TO MY MAUSER.

IN MARCH 1929, WHEN THE FIRST LOT OF BOMBS WAS READY, SUKHDEV, ONE OF THE REVOLUTIONARIES, CAME TO SEE AZAD AND BHAGAT SINGH.

AZAD, WE MUST TAKE SOME ACTION AGAINST THE INDUSTRIAL DISPUTES AND PUBLIC SECURITY ACTS.

WE CERTAINLY SHALL, WITH A BANG! WHY NOT THROW A BOMB IN THE ASSEMBLY? ONLY SUCH AN ACT WILL JOLT THE GOVERNMENT.

A GOOD IDEA.

I WILL HANDLE THIS JOB.

I WILL GO WITH YOU.

NO, DUTT, I WILL GO ALONE. I INTEND TO SACRIFICE MY LIFE.

THAT WILL NOT BE NECESSARY. I WILL MAKE ARRANGEMENTS FOR YOU TO ESCAPE.

BHAGAT SINGH, HOWEVER HAD OTHER IDEAS.

I MUST BE ARRESTED AND SENTENCED TO DEATH. IT WILL INSPIRE OTHERS TO DEDICATE THEIR LIVES TO THE CAUSE.

APRIL 8, 1929 WAS THE CHOSEN DATE. IN SPITE OF BHAGAT SINGH'S ATTEMPTS TO DISSUADE HIM, DUTT INSISTED ON GOING WITH HIM.

BOTH OF THEM WERE ARRESTED.

BHARAT MATA KI JAI!

MAY CAPITALIST IMPERIALISM BE DESTROYED.

WITHOUT BHAGAT SINGH, I AM LIKE A MAN WHO HAS LOST HIS RIGHT ARM.

I SUGGEST THAT OUR NEXT JOB SHOULD BE TO PLANT A BOMB UNDER LORD IRWIN'S TRAIN.

PLANS WERE MADE BUT BECAUSE OF SOME CHANGE IN TIMINGS THEY FELL THROUGH. A BOMB WAS DETONATED BUT THE VICEROY ESCAPED UNHARMED.

AZAD DISTRIBUTED PAMPHLETS WHICH EXPLAINED THE PHILOSOPHY OF THE BOMB.

WHY BOMBS? REVOLUTION ALONE WILL WIPE OUT CAPITALISM AND CLASS DIFFERENCES. IT WILL HELP ESTABLISH A NEW NATION AND A FREE PEOPLE.

EVERY ATTEMPT TO SAVE BHAGAT SINGH HAS FAILED. I WILL REST MY EFFORTS IN THAT DIRECTION FOR A WHILE. THE PARTY BADLY NEEDS MY ATTENTION. I MUST GO TO KANPUR.

AT KANPUR —

I HAVE JUST HEARD THE NEWS THAT SEVERAL OF OUR DELHI COMRADES HAVE TURNED TRAITORS.

I KNOW. OUR NUMBERS HAVE GROWN BUT OUR IDEALS HAVE FALLEN. THE TRAITORS WILL BE DEALT WITH.

I HAVE HAD MY OWN SUSPICIONS ABOUT CERTAIN COMRADES LIKE ··· ···WHERE WILL I FIND ANOTHER BHAGAT SINGH TODAY?

A FEW WEEKS LATER, AZAD HELD A MEETING AT DELHI.

WE ARE NO DOUBT SAD THAT WE HAVE NOT BEEN ABLE TO FREE BHAGAT SINGH. BUT WE WILL NOT LEAVE OUR WORK UNFINISHED. WE MUST CARRY ON.

BOMBS WERE MANUFACTURED AT DELHI AND KANPUR. AT NIGHTFALL EACH DAY—

ALL RIGHT. WE CAN STOP MAKING SOAP! LET US BEGIN WITH PICRIC ACID AND GUN COTTON.

HIMALAYA TOILETRIES

BRING OUT THE EXPLOSIVES. BEGIN WORKING ON THE BOMBS.

FUNDS WERE NEEDED TO RUN THESE CENTRES. DACOITY WAS ONCE AGAIN THE ONLY SOLUTION.

THE SHOP IS CLOSED. IT IS TEN O'CLOCK.

GADODIA STORES
CHANDNI CHOWK

WE KNOW THAT. GET OUT OF OUR WAY.

WE HAVE CUT THE TELEPHONE LINES.

THEY ENTERED THE SHOP. THE CLERK WAS COUNTING THE DAY'S TAKINGS.

HAND OVER ALL THE CASH.

HERE IS THE CASH AND ALL THE ORNAMENTS TOO.

KEEP THE ORNAMENTS. WE NEED ONLY THE CASH.

FROM ALLAHABAD, GOVERNMENT ARMS WERE SMUGGLED TO THE HEAD-QUARTERS WHICH WAS SHIFTED FROM DELHI TO KANPUR.

THE GOODS HAVE ARRIVED.

PUT THEM AWAY.

THE DAY THE BRITISH ARE KILLED BY THEIR OWN WEAPONS WILL BE THE HAPPIEST ONE FOR ME.

ONE MORNING, A FEW DAYS LATER —

HAVE YOU SEEN TODAY'S PAPERS? BHAGAT SINGH HAS BEEN SENTENCED TO DEATH.*

BHAGAT SINGH'S SACRIFICE WILL BE AN EXAMPLE FOR ALL OF US. WE TOO WILL DEDICATE OUR LIVES TO THE COUNTRY.

LATER, AT A MEETING —

AN ACHIEVEMENT! WE HAVE MADE OVER A HUNDRED BOMBS AT OUR KANPUR FACTORY. THEY ARE IN NO WAY INFERIOR TO STANDARD BOMBS.

WE WILL USE THEM AND DRIVE OUT THE FOREIGNERS, BUT ...

...WE CANNOT RELY ON ALL OUR COLLEAGUES. OUR IDEALS HAVE CEASED TO MEAN ANYTHING TO SOME OF THEM.

I THINK IT IS ADVISABLE TO REPEAL THE PARTY'S CONSTITUTION FOR A WHILE.

I TOO HAVE BEEN THINKING ABOUT IT. IN ORDER THAT THE AFFAIRS OF THE PARTY RUN SMOOTHLY, I PROPOSE TO SUSPEND THE CENTRAL COMMITTEE.

JUST THEN, AN ASSOCIATE OF AZAD WAS TALKING TO THE POLICE SUPERINTENDENT.

I WILL DELIVER AZAD TO YOU. I KNOW THE PLACES HE VISITS.

YOU WILL BE REWARDED, HANDSOMELY.

*BHAGAT SINGH WAS HANGED ON MARCH 23, 1931

HEADQUARTERS WERE NOW SHIFTED TO ALLAHABAD. ON FEBRUARY 27, 1931 AS AZAD AND SUKHDEVRAJ WERE ON THEIR WAY TO THE ALFRED PARK FROM MUIR COLLEGE—

THE RANKS OF TRUSTWORTHY MEMBERS HAVE DWINDLED. AND IT IS NOT WISE TO TRUST NEWCOMERS.

YOU ARE RIGHT. THE NEED FOR CAUTION HAS NEVER BEEN GREATER.

SUDDENLY—

LOOK! THERE GOES OUR 'COMRADE'. I ONLY HOPE THAT HE DIDN'T SEE

BUT THE 'COMRADE' HAD SEEN AZAD. HE CAME RUNNING TO THE POLICE STATION.

AZAD IS IN ALFRED PARK. START IMMEDIATELY.

AS THE BUGLE WAS SOUNDED, THE POLICEMEN TROOPED INTO THEIR VANS.

EIGHTY MEN IN FOUR VANS SPED TO ALFRED PARK.

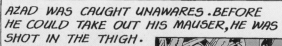

AZAD WAS CAUGHT UNAWARES. BEFORE HE COULD TAKE OUT HIS MAUSER, HE WAS SHOT IN THE THIGH.

PANDITJI!

THE NEXT MOMENT—

AZAD WAS SURROUNDED BY FORTY ARMED POLICEMEN WHO WERE SHOWERING BULLETS AT HIM.

✳ HONORIFIC USED WHILE ADDRESSING BRAHMANS

FOR THIRTY-TWO MINUTES AZAD HELD THEM AT BAY. THEN—

I HAVE ONLY ONE BULLET LEFT. NO! I WON'T BE TAKEN ALIVE!

HE RAISED HIS MAUSER TO HIS TEMPLE AND PRESSED THE TRIGGER.

AS AZAD FELL DEAD, THE POLICE CLOSED IN ON HIM. THE POLICE OFFICER ORDERED HIS MEN TO SHOOT AGAIN TO MAKE SURE THAT HE WAS DEAD. SO AFRAID WERE THE BRITISH EVEN OF AZAD'S CORPSE.

AZAD WAS ONLY TWENTY-FIVE WHEN HE BECAME A MARTYR IN THE CAUSE OF INDIAN INDEPENDENCE.

A COLLECTOR'S EDITION,
FROM INDIA'S FAVOURITE STORYTELLER.

India's greatest epic, told over 1,300 beautifully illustrated pages.
The Mahabharata Collector's Edition. It's not just a set of books, it's a piece of culture.

AMAR CHITRA KATHA

THE MAHABHARATA
COLLECTOR'S EDITION
Rupees Two thousand, four hundred and ninety-nine only.

BAGHA JATIN

THE 'TIGER' REVOLUTIONARY

The route to your roots

BAGHA JATIN

When a tiger attacked Jatin Mukherji, his friends felt sorry for the tiger! The animal was killed and Jatin spent only a short time in hospital recuperating from his wounds. The young man went on to display grit and determination to combat the worst of British colonialism in Bengal. He inspired his countrymen, who were in awe of their British masters, to stand tall and proud.

Script
Shanta Patil and Subba Rao

Illustrations
Souren Roy

Editor
Anant Pai

BAGHA JATIN

ABOUT NINETY YEARS AGO, IN THE VILLAGE KOYA OF BENGAL, A LITTLE BOY WAS BEING CHASED BY A STRAY DOG.

AS HE NEARED HIS HOUSE —

DON'T BE AFRAID! FACE HIM!

IT WAS HIS MOTHER WHO HAD CALLED OUT.

AS THE BOY STOPPED ABRUPTLY AND GLARED AT THE DOG, THE ANIMAL TURNED AND FLED.

HENCEFORTH, I'LL NEVER RUN AWAY FROM DANGER. I WILL STOP AND FIGHT.

THE LITTLE BOY, JATIN MUKHERJI, WAS DESTINED TO BECOME ONE OF THE GREATEST REVOLUTIONARIES OF INDIA.

JATIN WAS BORN IN 1879. HIS FATHER, UMESHCHANDRA MUKHERJI DIED WHEN JATIN WAS HARDLY FIVE YEARS OLD. AND HE WAS BROUGHT UP BY HIS MOTHER, A REMARKABLY STRONG WOMAN.

NEVER LET FEAR OVER-COME YOU, MY SON! FACE EVERY SITUATION WITH COURAGE AND DETERMINATION, AND YOU ARE BOUND TO WIN.

MY ENCOUNTER WITH THE DOG HAS TAUGHT ME THAT, MOTHER.

JATIN LOVED SWIMMING AND WAS AN EXPERT AT IT.

NO ONE CAN BEAT HIM.

SUDDENLY—

JATIN! THE WEEDS! TAKE CARE!

BUT THE WARNING WAS TOO LATE. JATIN GOT ENTANGLED IN THE WEEDS.

HIS PANIC-STRICKEN COMPANIONS GOT OUT OF THE WATER AND BROUGHT HIS MOTHER AND A FEW VILLAGERS TO THE SCENE.

JATIN, DON'T PANIC. WE ARE COMING TO HELP YOU.

NO! PLEASE DON'T! I MUST COME OUT OF THE WEEDS ON MY OWN.

AND I KNOW YOU WILL TACKLE THE WEEDS IN THE RIVER OF LIFE WITH THE SAME COURAGE, MY SON!

WITHOUT A DOUBT, MOTHER.

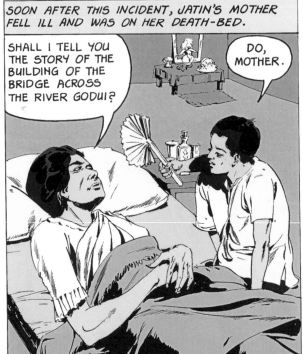

SOON AFTER THIS INCIDENT, JATIN'S MOTHER FELL ILL AND WAS ON HER DEATH-BED.

SHALL I TELL YOU THE STORY OF THE BUILDING OF THE BRIDGE ACROSS THE RIVER GODUI?

DO, MOTHER.

YOU WERE NOT EVEN BORN WHEN THE BRIDGE WAS BUILT.

"THE PEOPLE OF THE VILLAGE, EMPLOYED BY THE SAHIBS*, WORKED HARD."

* THE BRITISH IN INDIA WERE CALLED 'SAHIBS.'

"BUT WHEN THE RIVER SHOWED SIGNS OF SWELLING, THEY STOPPED WORK AND RAN TO THE SHORE."

" THE SAHIBS WERE ANGRY."

IF YOU RUN AGAIN, WE WILL SHOOT YOU DOWN.

" YET, WHEN THE HUGE WAVES ROSE, THEY STOPPED WORK AND RAN AGAIN. THEY WERE FIRED UPON. MANY FELL DEAD."

THEY DIED BECAUSE THEY WERE AFRAID TO RESIST THE RUTHLESS SAHIBS.

OUR PEOPLE ARE STILL AFRAID. LOVE THEM, JATIN. TEACH THEM TO BE COURAGEOUS.

I WILL, MOTHER.

AFTER THE DEATH OF HIS MOTHER, JATIN WENT TO CALCUTTA WHERE HE STAYED WITH HIS UNCLE. ONE DAY, AS HE WAS RETURNING HOME FROM SCHOOL —

WHAT'S GOING ON?

IT'S A GAME. CAN YOU SEE THE PURSE ON THE TABLE? IF YOU CAN GET PAST THE GUARD AND TAKE IT, IT'S YOURS.

THE NEXT MOMENT —

BRAVO!

HE'LL DO IT!

ONE DAY, JATIN HAPPENED TO WITNESS A STRANGE SCENE AT GORA BAZAR.

JATIN WALKED UP TO THE ENGLISHMAN.

JATIN SNATCHED THE STICK AND —

FIFTY! NOW THE CENSUS IS COMPLETE. GO HOME.

WITHOUT A WORD, THE ENGLISHMAN TOOK HIS ADVICE.

SOON A CROWD GATHERED AROUND JATIN.

GOOD WORK, MY SON. THE ENGLISHMAN WILL NOT REPEAT HIS LITTLE JOKE AGAIN.

WE CAN NOW VISIT THE BAZAR WITHOUT FEAR.

WHY DIDN'T YOU STOP HIM WHEN HE FIRST STARTED THIS GAME?

HOW COULD WE?

HE IS AN ENGLISHMAN.

THE FEAR OF THE ENGLISHMAN MUST BE REMOVED FROM THE MINDS OF OUR PEOPLE. THEY MUST BE SHOWN THAT THE ENGLISHMAN CAN BE FOUGHT AND DEFEATED.

IN 1905 WHEN THE PRINCE OF WALES VISITED INDIA, SIX YOUNG ENGLISHMEN WERE ON THE LOOKOUT FOR A PLACE FROM WHERE THEY COULD HAVE A CLEAR VIEW OF THE PROCESSION.

LET'S SIT ATOP THAT COACH.

YOU COULDN'T HAVE FOUND A BETTER VANTAGE POINT!

HELLO, BEAUTIFUL!

WILL YOU DANCE WITH ME, MY PRETTY MAID?

MA, WE SHOULDN'T HAVE COME. LET'S GO HOME.

DARLING, WON'T YOU TAKE US WITH YOU AND ENTERTAIN US?

I'LL ENTERTAIN YOU, YOU ROGUES!

IT WAS JATIN.

AND JATIN GAVE THE ILL-MANNERED YOUTHS THE ENTERTAINMENT OF THEIR LIVES!

REMARKABLE! SIX ENGLISHMEN! AND YOU CHASED THEM AWAY SINGLE-HANDED!

IF WE JOINED HANDS, WE COULD CHASE THE WHOLE LOT OF THEM OUT OF OUR COUNTRY!

I'VE KILLED THE TIGER BUT I DO NEED HELP —A DOCTOR'S HELP!

WELL DONE, BAGHA* JATIN!

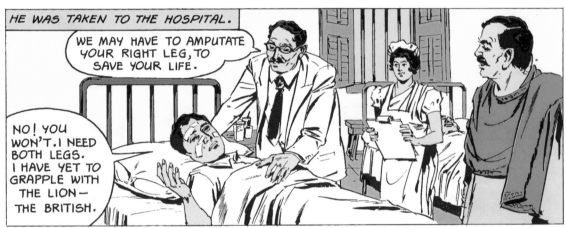

HE WAS TAKEN TO THE HOSPITAL.

WE MAY HAVE TO AMPUTATE YOUR RIGHT LEG, TO SAVE YOUR LIFE.

NO! YOU WON'T. I NEED BOTH LEGS. I HAVE YET TO GRAPPLE WITH THE LION — THE BRITISH.

JATIN CAME OUT OF THE HOSPITAL WITHOUT LOSING A LIMB.

YOU ARE A FIGHTER, INDEED. YOU HUMBLED THE TIGER FIRST AND THEN DEATH ITSELF!

BUT TO DO THE HAT TRICK, I MUST SUCCEED IN HUMBLING THE BRITISH, DOCTOR.

* TIGER

ONCE, WHEN HE WAS TRAVELLING IN A TRAIN—

PLEASE LEAVE MY POOR GIRL ALONE.

SHUT UP, GRANDPA.

WHY ARE YOU SHY, DARLING?

THE SCOUNDRELS!

WITH A ROAR, JATIN BENT THE BARS THAT SHIELDED THEM...

...AND CHARGED.

WE ARE GRATEFUL TO YOU, MY SON. YOU HAVE SAVED OUR HONOUR.

BUT THE HONOUR OF MOTHER INDIA WILL BE SAFE ONLY WHEN WE'VE THROWN OFF THE YOKE OF BRITISH RULE.

WE SHARE YOUR SENTIMENTS. MAY GOD BE WITH YOU. BUT TAKE CARE, SON.

SOON AFTER THAT, JATIN WAS ARRESTED AND BROUGHT BEFORE A BRITISH JUDGE FOR HUMBLING FOUR INSOLENT BRITISH SOLDIERS.

FOUR ROBUST BRITISH OFFICERS PROVED HELPLESS AGAINST ONE NATIVE!

YE..S, SIR —

THIS TRIAL, IF IT GOES ON, WILL RECEIVE PUBLICITY. OUR MEN IN INDIA WILL BE DEMORALIZED. OTHER NATIVES MAY TAKE A CUE FROM THIS INCIDENT.

YOUR LORDSHIP, PERMIT US TO WITHDRAW THE CASE.

PERMISSION GRANTED. CASE DISMISSED.

MEANWHILE, JATIN HAD TAKEN UP A JOB AS A STENOGRAPHER TO THE GOVERNOR'S SECRETARY.

HOW COULD YOU, A STAUNCH NATION-ALIST, WORK FOR THE BRITISH GOVERNMENT?

BECAUSE IT PROVIDES ME WITH A PERFECT COVER. NOBODY WOULD SUSPECT ME.

JATIN TRAINED YOUNG MEN IN THE USE OF FIRE-ARMS.

HE TAUGHT THEM HOW TO MANU-FACTURE HAND-MADE BOMBS...

...AND THROW THEM AT BRITISH OFFICERS.

BUT THE BRITISH POLICE OFFICERS WERE NOT PERTURBED. THEY HAD THEIR REASONS.

WE HAVE ARRESTED AUROBINDO GHOSH. THIS MIGHT PROVE TO BE THE DEATH-KNELL OF THE SO-CALLED REVOLUTION.

WITH THEIR LEADER BEHIND BARS, THE YOUNGSTERS WILL BE DEMORALIZED.

THE NEXT DAY AT THE COURT AS THE GOVERNMENT PLEADER, ASHU BISWAS, ROSE TO ARGUE THE CASE AGAINST AUROBINDO, A BULLET HIT HIM.

A-A-AH!

MAY THIS BE A LESSON TO ALL SUCH TRAITORS.

THE REVOLUTIONARY WHO KILLED THE GOVERNMENT PLEADER WAS HANGED. BUT THE SPATE OF KILLINGS DID NOT ABATE.

WE MUST BE EXTRA VIGILANT, ALUM.

I'VE WARNED EVERY SENIOR OFFICER NOT TO MOVE WITHOUT AN ESCORT.

IN SPITE OF THE PRECAUTIONS TAKEN, THE ANTI-NATIONALIST POLICE SUPERINTENDENT, SAMUEL ALUM, WAS SHOT DEAD, RIGHT ON THE STEPS OF THE HIGH COURT.

TEGART, THE COMMISSIONER OF POLICE WAS NATURALLY WORRIED.

TO BE HONEST WITH YOU, BIRD, I'M BAFFLED. NO SOONER IS ONE REBEL NABBED THAN ANOTHER SPRINGS UP!

THAT'S BECAUSE WE'VE NOT YET CAUGHT THE BRAIN BEHIND IT ALL.

AND IT IS MY BELIEF THAT JATIN IS THE MAN.

JATIN? QUITE POSSIBLE. BUT DO YOU HAVE PROOF?

I'LL HAVE IT SOON. MY MEN WILL MAKE ONE OF THOSE ARRESTED REVOLUTIONARIES TALK.

AS SOON AS TEGART LEFT, BIRD CALLED IN ONE OF HIS OFFICERS.

HAVE ANY OF THEM TALKED?

NOT YET, SIR. TORTURE HAS PROVED USELESS. I'VE DECIDED TO CHANGE MY TACTICS.

LATER, AT THE PRISON CELL—

I'M GOING TO SET YOU FREE. DO YOU KNOW WHY? BECAUSE BAGHA IS WAITING TO KILL YOU.

THE OFFICER PRODUCED A RIGGED COPY OF 'YUGANTAR', THE NEWS-LETTER OF THE REVOLUTIONARIES.

READ IT FOR YOURSELF. JATIN HAS DENOUNCED YOU AS A TRAITOR AND ACCUSES YOU OF TURNING INFORMER TO US— THE POLICE. HE IS SURE TO KILL YOU.

THE REVOLUTIONARY FELL INTO THE TRAP.

HOW COULD YOU, DADA*?

SO THE CAT IS OUT OF THE BAG! JATIN IS YOUR LEADER!

* JATIN WAS ADDRESSED AS "DADA"— THE ELDER BROTHER.

AS THE JUBILANT OFFICER WALKED AWAY —

OH, I HAVE BEEN TRICKED! DADA, I HAVE LET YOU DOWN. FORGIVE ME, DADA.

JATIN WAS ARRESTED AND SUBJECTED TO TORTURE.

AMAZING. HE WON'T CONFESS, HE WON'T CRY OUT, AND HE WON'T EVEN COMPLAIN!

I AM BEGINNING TO FEEL ASHAMED OF WHAT I'M DOING.

THEY CHANGED THEIR TACTICS.

BECOME ONE OF US. YOU'LL HAVE A LARGE PURSE, A FINE MANSION, THE FINEST OF WINES AND THE PRETTIEST OF WOMEN.

THE MAN WHO HAD REMAINED SILENT THROUGHOUT HIS ORDEALS, NOW ALL BUT ROARED.

SHUT UP!

FIFTEEN MONTHS LATER, JATIN WAS SET FREE FOR WANT OF PROOF.

YOU'RE NO LONGER WORKING FOR THE GOVERNMENT, I HEARD.

I'M NOT. I'M GOING INTO BUSINESS. THAT'S MY FIRM — BUILDERS AND CONTRACTORS.

BUILDERS & CONTRACTORS

AFTER HIS RELEASE FROM PRISON, WHEN AUROBINDO LEFT CALCUTTA FOR PONDI-CHERRY, JATIN ASSUMED THE LEADERSHIP OF THE REVOLUTIONARIES.

HOW IS THE BUILDING WORK GOING ON IN THE PUNJAB?

OUR PEOPLE ARE ASKING FOR MORE MATERIALS.

WE ARE DOING OUR BEST. WE ARE IMPORTING MATERIALS FROM RUSSIA, GERMANY AND JAPAN.

TO SMUGGLE ARMS INTO THE COUNTRY UNDER THE VERY NOSE OF THE GOVERNMENT, THE REVOLUTIONARIES SET UP A COMPANY.

HARRY & CO.
EXPORTERS & IMPORTERS

THE REVOLUTIONARIES WERE AT LAST READY.

FEBRUARY 21, 1915. THAT'S THE DAY WE STRIKE. THE FIRST SHOT WILL BE FIRED IN THE PUNJAB, RASHBIHARI.

BUT THE FIRST SHOT WAS NEVER HEARD IN THE PUNJAB. ONE OF THE REVOLUTIONARIES TURNED TRAITOR AND RASHBIHARI BOSE HAD TO FLEE TO JAPAN. THE CAPTURED REVOLUTIONARIES CHEERFULLY WENT TO THE GALLOWS.

THE POLICE OFFICIALS AT CALCUTTA BECAME ALERT.

THEY FAILED IN THE PUNJAB. I WON'T ALLOW THEM TO SUCCEED IN BENGAL.

THEN WE MUST PUT JATIN BEHIND BARS.

THERE WAS A FRANTIC SEARCH FOR HIM IN CALCUTTA.

BUILDERS & CONTRACTORS

OUR BIRD HAS FLOWN.

BUT WHERE TO? WHAT IS HE UP TO?

THEY SOON FOUND OUT.

HERE IS AN INTEREST-ING LETTER FROM HARRY AND CO. TO UNIVERSAL EMPORIUM AT BALASORE TOWN.*

WHAT DOES IT SAY?

IT IS AN ADVICE TO COLLECT SHIPMENT AT THE USUAL PLACE.

SHIPMENT? COULD IT BE ARMS?

PRECISELY. THOSE ARMS WERE MEANT FOR UNIVERSAL EMPORIUM — THAT IS FOR JATIN.

YOU COULD BE RIGHT. GO TO BALASORE AND INVESTIGATE.

AT UNIVERSAL EMPORIUM —

WE HAVE SEARCH-ED THE PLACE THOROUGHLY. WE HAVEN'T UNEARTH-ED A SINGLE CLUE.

* IN ORISSA

WHEN THEY WERE ABOUT TO GIVE UP —

SIR! A PIECE OF PAPER... WITH JUST ONE WORD... KAPTIPADA.

WHERE IS THIS KAPTIPADA, MR. KILBY?

ABOUT THIRTY MILES FROM HERE. IT MAKES AN IDEAL HIDEOUT.

MR. KILBY WAS THE DISTRICT MAGISTRATE OF BALASORE.

THE POLICE WERE ON THE RIGHT TRACK. JATIN, WITH TWO YOUNG LIEUTENANTS, WAS HIDING AT AN ESTATE NEAR KAPTIPADA; WHILE TWO OTHERS KEPT WATCH, SIX MILES AWAY FROM THE HIDEOUT. IT WAS JATIN WHO SPOTTED THE POLICE.

WE WILL SOON HAVE COMPANY.

THE POLICE SWOOPED DOWN ON THE ESTATE.

LOOK! A TARGET FOR SHOOTING PRACTICE!

I THINK WE'VE COME TO THE RIGHT PLACE.

THEY QUESTIONED MANINDRA CHAKRA-
VARTY WHO HAD SECURED THE PLACE
FOR JATIN.

I KNOW NOTHING,
MASTER. THE
BABUS* HAVE
GONE OUT ON A
HUNT.

HE HAS
ESCAPED
AGAIN.

LET US ANNOUNCE THAT DANGER-
OUS DACOITS ARE AT LARGE, AND
THAT A REWARD OF TEN THOU-
SAND RUPEES AWAITS ANYONE
WHO COMES FORWARD WITH
USEFUL INFORMATION
ABOUT THEM.

LEAVING THE GUARDS THERE, KILBY AND
BIRD RETURNED TO BALASORE.

THAT NIGHT, JATIN CALLED ON MANINDRA.

DADA, WHY DID
YOU COME BACK?
THEY ARE ON
THE LOOKOUT
FOR YOU.

I KNOW. I CAME TO
TAKE LEAVE OF YOU
AND TO THANK YOU
FOR ALL THAT YOU
HAVE DONE. GOOD-
BYE, BROTHER!

HE RISKED HIS LIFE
JUST TO THANK ME.
I HOPE HE COMES
THROUGH THIS
ORDEAL UN-
SCATHED.

* TERM USED IN BENGAL FOR ADDRESSING MEN OF GOOD SOCIAL STANDING

24

JATIN'S COMPANIONS, CHITTAPRIYA AND MANORANJAN WANTED THEIR LEADER TO LEAVE THEM BEHIND AND ESCAPE.

DADA, DON'T WORRY ABOUT US. TAKE CARE OF YOURSELF.

YOU CAN MOVE FASTER WITHOUT US.

IGNORING THEIR SUGGESTIONS, JATIN TOOK THEM ALONG WITH HIM. THEY JOINED THE TWO OTHER LIEUTENANTS — NIREN AND JYOTISH — WHO WERE CAMPING SIX MILES AWAY. AND THE FIVE OF THEM MARCHED OUT INTO THE NIGHT.

BY DAWN THE ENTIRE REGION WAS AGOG WITH THE NEWS OF THE ESCAPED DACOITS.

10,000 RUPEES IF ANYONE CATCHES THEM.

I COULD USE THAT MONEY.

JUST THEN JATIN AND HIS COMPANIONS ARRIVED THERE AFTER AN ARDUOUS TREK.

WILL YOU KINDLY TAKE US ACROSS THE RIVER?

DA... DACOITS!

A CROWD SOON COLLECTED ON THE BANKS.

BELIEVE US, FRIENDS. WE ARE NOT DACOITS. PLEASE FERRY US ACROSS.

YOU LIARS!

CHEAT ME OF MY 10,000 RUPEES, WILL YOU?

JUST THEN MANORANJAN FIRED A FEW BLANK SHOTS.

DON'T TRY TO STOP THEM! THEY'LL KILL US.

LET THEM GO.

THE FIVE WALKED A MILE. THEY HAD HAD NEITHER FOOD NOR SLEEP FOR MORE THAN SIXTY HOURS. SUDDENLY —

LOOK!

THEY WALKED UP TO THE SHOP AND BOUGHT SOME FOOD.

I HAVE NO CHANGE, BABU!

NEVER MIND. KEEP THE NOTE.

26

TEN RUPEES MEANS NOTHING TO THEM! WHO COULD THEY BE? DACOITS!

DACOITS! DACOITS!

HIS SHOUTS SOON DREW A CROWD. WHEN A POLICE OFFICER TRIED TO ARREST JATIN, HE WAS BODILY LIFTED AND THROWN AT THE CROWD.

IN THE COMMOTION THAT ENSUED, THEY ESCAPED AND SWAM ACROSS THE RIVER, HOLDING THEIR AMMUNITION HIGH.

WHEN THEY REACHED THE OPPOSITE BANK—

DO YOU SEE THAT HILLOCK? THAT'S WHERE WE'LL FIGHT OUR LAST BATTLE.

DADA, EVEN NOW IT IS NOT TOO LATE. YOU MUST ESCAPE.

DADA, FOR THE SAKE OF THE COUNTRY YOU MUST SAVE YOUR LIFE.

DON'T WORRY. IF ONE JATIN FALLS A THOUSAND MORE WILL RISE.

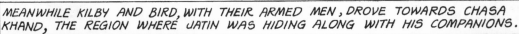

MEANWHILE KILBY AND BIRD, WITH THEIR ARMED MEN, DROVE TOWARDS CHASA KHAND, THE REGION WHERE JATIN WAS HIDING ALONG WITH HIS COMPANIONS.

THE POLICE PARTY ADVANCED, SHOOTING THEIR WAY FORWARD.

WHY DON'T THEY RESPOND?

PERHAPS THEY HAVE NO BULLETS.

BUT THE POLICE WERE MISTAKEN. THE NEXT MOMENT —

AH!

THE POLICE SUFFERED HEAVY LOSSES. CHITTA-PRIYA WAS SHOT DEAD. JATIN DREW HIS DEAD COMPANION'S HEAD ONTO HIS LAP AND CONTINUED TO SHOOT.

SUDDENLY ALL WAS QUIET.

I THINK THEY HAVE EXHAUSTED THEIR BULLETS.

WHEN THE POLICE REACHED THE TOP OF THE HILLOCK —

OH GOD! WHAT A GHASTLY SIGHT!

MR. KILBY BROUGHT WATER IN HIS HELMET.

DRINK THIS, MR. MUKHERJI. YOU'LL FEEL BETTER.

THANKS.

IT STARTED TO RAIN. MR. KILBY COVERED JATIN WITH HIS COAT.

THE CAPTIVES WERE TAKEN TO THE HOSPITAL AT BALASORE. ON THE WAY —

ARE YOU SAYING SOMETHING, MR. MUKHERJI?

YES. I ALONE AM RESPONSIBLE FOR ALL THAT HAS HAPPENED. SEE THAT NO INJUSTICE IS DONE TO THESE BOYS.

JATIN, WHO HAD BEEN WOUNDED, HAD TO BE OPERATED UPON. TEGART, THE POLICE COMMISSIONER RUSHED FROM CALCUTTA TO BALASORE.

TELL ME, MUKHERJI, WHAT...CAN I DO ...FOR YOU?

JATIN SMILED.

NOTHING, THANK YOU. IT'S ALL OVER. GOODBYE.

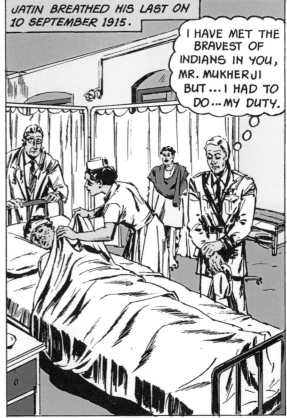

JATIN BREATHED HIS LAST ON 10 SEPTEMBER 1915.

I HAVE MET THE BRAVEST OF INDIANS IN YOU, MR. MUKHERJI BUT...I HAD TO DO...MY DUTY.

21 Inspiring Stories of Courage

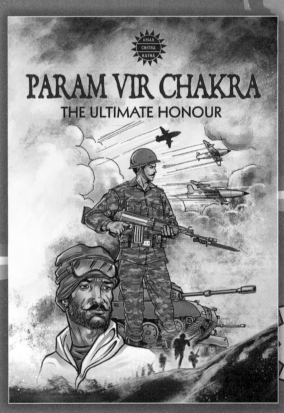

DESHBANDHU CHITTARANJAN DAS

HE SACRIFICED HIS ALL FOR THE COUNTRY

The route to your roots

DESHBANDHU CHITTARANJAN DAS

Brilliant lawyer, talented poet, farsighted statesman - Chittaranjan Das had all it takes to make life prosperous and peaceful, but he chose hardship and suffering for 'he dreamed and thought and talked of the freedom of India, and of nothing else.' In return, he received in abundance the undying gratitude and love from his countrymen. Deshbandhu is remembered to this day for his matchless service and sacrifice.

Script	Illustrations	Editor
H.Atmaram	Souren Roy	Anant Pai

Cover illustration by: Ramesh Umrotkar

Grateful thanks to the Deshbandhu Chittaranjan Das Memorial Committee, Kolkata, for visual references and authentication of script.

DESHBANDHU CHITTARANJAN DAS

CHITTARANJAN DAS WAS BORN IN CALCUTTA ON NOVEMBER 5, 1870, IN A FAMILY OF EMINENT LAWYERS. WHEN HE WAS 20, HE GRADUATED WITH DISTINCTION FROM CALCUTTA UNIVERSITY.

SO IT WAS NATURAL THAT HIS FATHER SHOULD WANT HIM TO BECOME AN I.C.S. OFFICER.

CHITTO, YOU WILL GO TO LONDON FOR THE I.C.S. EXAMINATION.

BUT... FATHER... WE CAN'T AFFORD THAT... YOUR DEBTS...

DON'T WORRY, SON. I HAVE SET ASIDE ENOUGH FOR YOUR EXPENSES!

AND SO CHITTARANJAN ARRIVED IN LONDON IN 1890...

...AND BEGAN STUDYING FOR HIS I.C.S. EXAMINATION.

ONE DAY IN 1892 —

DAS, HAVE YOU HEARD THE LATEST? THE LIBERAL PARTY HAS CHOSEN DADABHAI NAOROJI AS ONE OF ITS CANDIDATES FOR THE PARLIAMENTARY ELECTION.

THAT'S GREAT NEWS!

HE MUST WIN. IT WOULD MEAN A STRONG VOICE FOR INDIA IN THE BRITISH PARLIAMENT.

DAS TOOK AN ACTIVE INTEREST IN THE ELECTION CAMPAIGN. AROUND THAT TIME LORD SALISBURY, A MINISTER, REFERRED TO DADABHAI AS "THAT BLACK MAN".

DAS STRONGLY CONDEMNED THE STATEMENT AT A MEETING OF THE LIBERAL PARTY.

...LET ME REPEAT — THE HONOURABLE MINISTER IS WELL WITHIN HIS RIGHTS TO CRITICIZE THE POLICIES OF HIS OPPONENT, BUT NOT HIS PERSON.

IN FACT HE WHOM THE MINISTER CALLS "BLACK" IS A SHADE FAIRER THAN THE MINISTER HIMSELF!

AND A FAR FINER PERSON TOO!

DADABHAI NAOROJI, THE FOUNDER OF THE FRIENDS OF INDIA SOCIETY, WAS A POPULAR AND RESPECTED PERSONALITY ON THE BRITISH POLITICAL AND SOCIAL SCENE. BUT HE LOST THE ELECTION BY A NARROW MARGIN.

AND ACTIVE PARTICIPATION IN POLITICS COST CHITTARANJAN HIS ENTRY INTO THE CIVIL SERVICE. THE DAY THE RESULTS WERE ANNOUNCED —

THE CIVIL SERVICE DOES NOT WANT ME. HOW DISAPPOINTED FATHER WILL BE!

BUT IF HIS FATHER WAS DISAPPOINTED, HE DID NOT SHOW IT IN THE LETTER HE WROTE TO DAS.

...NEVER MIND, CHITTO. DO NOT BE DISHEARTENED. TAKE UP LAW. YOU WERE BORN IN A FAMILY OF LAWYERS.

DAS TOOK HIS FATHER'S ADVICE, WAS CALLED TO THE BAR THE SAME YEAR, AND SET SAIL FOR INDIA IN 1893.

WHEN HE GOT HOME —

IT'S GOOD TO HAVE YOU BACK, CHITTO.

BUT YOU DON'T LOOK YOUR OLD SELF, FATHER.

IT'S YOUR DEBTS. THEY'VE WORN YOU DOWN.

BUT THEY WON'T ANY MORE, NOW THAT YOU ARE HERE TO TAKE CARE OF EVERYTHING.

DAS STARTED PRACTICE AT THE CALCUTTA COURT. THE FIRST DAYS WERE A STRUGGLE. HE HAD TO WAIT FOR CLIENTS.

IN THOSE DAYS LAWYERS HAD THEIR OWN CARRIAGES. BUT DAS COULD NOT AS YET AFFORD ONE!

ONE TICKET TO ESPLANADE, PLEASE.

HE USUALLY WENT TO THE COURT BY TRAM AND RETURNED HOME ON FOOT.

ONE EVENING —

CAN I GIVE YOU A LIFT, DAS?

NO, THANK YOU! I FIND WALKING GOOD FOR MY HEALTH.

GRADUALLY, HOWEVER, HIS PRACTICE IMPROVED.

BABU, YOU MUST TAKE UP MY CASE.

LET ME STUDY IT.

BUT IN 1896 A FRESH CONTINGENCY AROSE AT HOME.

I AM DEEP IN DEBT AS IT IS. AND NOW THIS.

WHAT, FATHER?

I STOOD A MAN THIRTY THOUSAND RUPEES IN SURETY AND THE FELLOW HAS VANISHED ! HIS CREDITORS TOO WILL PESTER US. WE'LL HAVE NO PEACE.

THERE IS ONLY ONE THING WE CAN DO.

WE WILL JOINTLY FILE AN INSOLVENCY PETITION

NO ! NO ! NOT THAT !

IMAGINE THE DISGRACE. PEOPLE WILL SHUN US. YOUR PRACTICE WILL BE RUINED.

FATHER, IF MY CLIENTS ARE CONVINCED THAT I AM A COMPETENT BARRISTER, THEY WILL CONTINUE TO COME TO ME !

HIS FATHER RELUCTANTLY GAVE IN.

THE PETITION WAS FILED, THE CASE ADMITTED AND THE DECREE OF INSOLVENCY ISSUED.

FATHER'S CREDITORS WILL BE UNHAPPY WITH THE AMOUNT THEY'LL GET AFTER THE COURT AUCTIONS OUR ESTATES AND EFFECTS. I MUST WORK HARD AND ONE DAY MAKE GOOD THEIR LOSSES.

IN SPITE OF THESE PRESSURES, DAS FOUND TIME TO WRITE POETRY, A PURSUIT HE EXCELLED IN AND ENJOYED. HIS FIRST ANTHOLOGY OF POEMS, MALANCHA, WAS PUBLISHED IN 1896.

POEM OF DESHBANDHU IN HIS OWN HANDWRITING

THE TONE OF ITS CONTENTS HOWEVER WAS TOO RADICAL EVEN FOR THE REFORMIST BRAHMO SAMAJ TO WHICH HE BELONGED.

HIS WORKS CLEARLY INDICATE THAT HE HAS NO REGARD FOR BRAHMO IDEALS NOR RESPECT FOR THE VIEWS OF ITS ELDERS.

AROUND THIS TIME, DAS'S MARRIAGE WAS FIXED. PIQUED BY THE YOUNG MAN'S CRITICISM, THE ACHARYAS OF BRAHMO SAMAJ DECIDED TO BOYCOTT THE WEDDING. BUT DAS INSISTED THAT THEY HEAR HIM OUT BEFORE THEY DID.

...AND SO I CONCLUDE—WE BRAHMO SAMAJISTS CALL OURSELVES REFORMISTS*. IS THIS THE WAY ENLIGHTENED REFORMISTS REACT TO CRITICISM?

DAS WON THE DAY AND WAS MARRIED TO BASANTI DEVI IN 1897, ACCORDING TO BRAHMO RITES, WITH THE ACHARYAS AS WITNESSES.

✻ a person who works to change things from within society

IN 1905, THE BRITISH PARTITIONED BENGAL ON COMMUNAL LINES. THERE WAS A STRONG REACTION FROM THE PEOPLE.

BENGAL IS ONE. HINDUS AND MUSLIMS ARE ONE.

VANDE MATARAM!

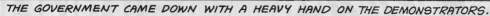

THE GOVERNMENT CAME DOWN WITH A HEAVY HAND ON THE DEMONSTRATORS.

SEVERAL YOUNG MEN SERIOUSLY THOUGHT OF RESORTING TO ARMS TO OVERTHROW THE BRITISH GOVERNMENT. THEY LOOKED TO AUROBINDO FOR GUIDANCE.

DAS WAS, FOR SOME TIME, ASSOCIATED WITH THESE REVOLUTIONARIES.

BUT HE HAD PRACTICALLY GIVEN UP ACTIVE POLITICS TO CONCENTRATE ON HIS LEGAL CAREER. AND THERE HIS REPUTATION STEADILY GAINED GROUND AND SO DID HIS INCOME! HE WAS EQUALLY SUCCESSFUL IN CIVIL AND CRIMINAL CASES, AND EARNED FAME FOR HIS SKILL IN CROSS EXAMINATION.

MEANWHILE THE GOVERNMENT HAD TAKEN SEVERAL STEPS TO CURB THE ACTIVITIES OF THE REVOLUTIONARIES. ONE DAY —

DAS! AUROBINDO TOO HAS BEEN TAKEN INTO CUSTODY IN CONNECTION WITH THE ALIPORE CONSPIRACY.

WHAT!

GHOSE TOO ARRESTED! AND WITH BARELY ANY FUNDS FOR DEFENCE!

KNOWING THIS DAS ACCEPTED THE BRIEF EVEN THOUGH IT MEANT A SET-BACK IN HIS OWN INCOME, ANOTHER ROUND OF BORROWING, AND HARDSHIP FOR THE FAMILY. NIGHT AND DAY HE PORED OVER HIS LAW BOOKS OBLIVIOUS OF ALL ELSE. THE TRIAL BEGAN IN 1908...

...AND WENT ON FOR SEVERAL MONTHS. HIS CONCLUDING ADDRESS TO THE JURY ITSELF TOOK NINE DAYS! PRESENTED IN THE FIRST PERSON, IT HAD TAKEN INTO ACCOUNT THE SOUL OF AUROBINDO.

... DO NOT IMPUTE TO ME CRIMES I AM NOT GUILTY OF, DEEDS AGAINST WHICH MY WHOLE NATURE REVOLTS AND WHICH, HAVING REGARD TO MY MENTAL CAPACITY, IS SOMETHING WHICH COULD NEVER HAVE BEEN PERPETRATED BY ME. IF IT IS AN OFFENCE TO PREACH THE IDEAL OF FREEDOM, I ADMIT HAVING DONE IT... YOU WILL NEVER GET OUT OF ME A DENIAL OF THAT CHARGE...

HE HAS ACTED AGAINST THE LAW OF THE LAND!

THE WHOLE EDIFICE OF BRITISH RULE IS BASED ON BRUTE FORCE AND HAS NO MORAL SANCTION.

FINALLY HE SUMMED UP.

MY APPEAL TO YOU THEREFORE IS THAT A MAN LIKE THIS... STANDS TRIAL NOT ONLY BEFORE THIS BAR, BUT BEFORE THE HIGH COURT OF HISTORY. LONG AFTER THIS CONTROVERSY IS HUSHED... THE WORLD WILL LOOK UPON HIM AS A PROPHET OF NATIONALISM AND A LOVER OF HUMANITY.

THE SPELLBOUND JURY GAVE ITS VERDICT AND AUROBINDO WAS AQUITTED IN MAY 1909.

THE CASE WON DAS INTERNATIONAL ACCLAIM AS ONE OF THE FOREMOST BARRISTERS IN THE WORLD AND NATIONAL ACCLAIM AS A GREAT PATRIOT.

HIS SELFLESS WORK OF THE PAST FEW MONTHS PAID HIM RICH, THOUGH UNSOUGHT, DIVIDENDS. HIS REPUTATION SOARED AND SO DID HIS INCOME. HE NOW OWNED A CARRIAGE AND LIVED IN STYLE.

THE TIME HAD COME TO FULFIL THE VOW HE HAD MADE TO HIMSELF YEARS AGO.

PLEASE MAKE A LIST OF ALL MY FATHER'S CREDITORS, AND THEIR DUES.

BUT, CHITTO, YOUR FATHER AND YOU WERE DECLARED INSOLVENT. YOU ARE NOT LEGALLY BOUND TO REPAY THOSE DEBTS!

PERHAPS NOT, LEGALLY — BUT DEFINITELY SO, MORALLY! THEY HELPED MY FATHER WHEN HE WAS IN NEED.

A FEW DAYS LATER THE MAN WAS BACK.

YOUR JOB IS DONE! I HAVE SPOKEN TO SOME OF THE CREDITORS AND THEY HAVE AGREED TO REDUCE THEIR CLAIMS.

BUT I DID NOT ASK YOU TO DO THAT! I WILL CLEAR MY FATHER'S DEBTS IN FULL AND WITH INTEREST.

ONE WHO LEAST EXPECTED THE CHEQUE HE RECEIVED, WAS S.R. MULLICK, A CHILDHOOD FRIEND. HIS FATHER HAD ONCE LENT DAS'S FATHER SOME MONEY!

WHAT IS THIS?

CHITTO IS SYSTEMATICALLY CLEARING OLD DEBTS.

RETURNING MONEY MY FATHER LENT HIS FATHER! HMMPH! WOULD I HAVE DONE THE SAME? I WONDER...

ON NO FRONT DID DAS LET THE TEMPTATION OF MONEY DESTROY HIS LOFTY VALUES OR HIS DEEP LOVE FOR HIS MOTHERLAND AND THOSE WHO FOUGHT TO FREE HER.

I CANNOT TAKE UP YOUR CASE. I HAVE TO GO TO CHITTAGONG* TO DEFEND SOME POLITICAL PRISONERS.

BUT, SIR, WE DEPEND ON YOU. WE'LL PAY YOU RS. 25,000 AS A RETAINER!

THEN YOU CAN EASILY GET ANOTHER GOOD LAWYER. MY PENNILESS CLIENTS OUT THERE CAN'T. I MUST GO TO THEM. I AM SORRY.

NOT ONLY DID HE GIVE PRIORITY TO PATRIOTS BUT OFTEN DIPPED INTO HIS OWN BANK BALANCE WHEN HE TOOK UP THEIR CASES!

* CHITTAGONG — NOW IN BANGLADESH

11

NO LESS GENEROUS WAS HE TO THE NEEDY. AND IN SUCH CASES HE PREFERRED TO REMAIN ANONYMOUS. ONE MORNING AS HE WAS ABOUT TO LEAVE FOR THE COURT HE SAW AN OLD MAN AT THE GATE.

ARE YOU WAITING FOR SOMEBODY?

I WANT TO MEET CHITTARANJAN BABU. I DESPERATELY NEED SOME MONEY AND I HAVE HEARD MUCH ABOUT HIS GENE-ROSITY.

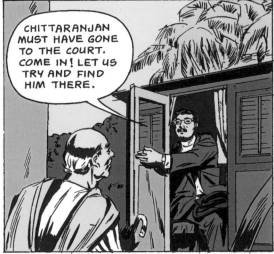

CHITTARANJAN MUST HAVE GONE TO THE COURT. COME IN! LET US TRY AND FIND HIM THERE.

WHEN THEY REACHED THE COURT —

PLEASE WAIT HERE. I'LL FIND HIM AND SEND HIM TO YOU.

A LITTLE LATER, A CHAPRASSI CAME TO THE OLD MAN WITH A CHEQUE.

THIS IS FOR YOU. DAS MOSHAY HAS SENT IT.

BUT HE HAS NOT EVEN SEEN ME! TAKE ME TO HIM! I WANT TO THANK HIM!

THE CHAPRASSI LED HIM TO DAS.

OH! IT WAS YOU!

DIDN'T I TELL YOU NOT TO...

IT'S NOT HIS FAULT, SIR. I INSISTED ON SEEING YOU.

DO YOU THINK I COULD ACCEPT HELP WITHOUT THANKING MY BENEFACTOR?

MAY GOD BLESS YOU, SON!

BY THE YEAR 1918 DAS HAD BEGUN TO TAKE AN ACTIVE INTEREST IN THE NATIONAL MOVEMENT. HE ADDRESSED SEVERAL MEETINGS.

INDIA SHOULD BECOME SELF-RELIANT. WE SHOULD MEET THE WEST AS EQUALS!

INSTEAD THE ROWLATT BILL * WAS PASSED AND EVEN PEACEFUL UNARMED PERSONS WERE LATHI-CHARGED...

...AND IMPRISONED....

...OR SHOWERED WITH BULLETS AS IN THE SHAMEFUL, MINDLESS MASSACRE OF INNOCENTS ORDERED BY GENERAL DYER AT JALLIANWALA BAUGH IN 1919.

THE PROPOSAL THAT DAS BE PERMITTED TO ATTEND THE SUBSEQUENT OFFICIAL ENQUIRY CONDUCTED BY THE BRITISH WAS REJECTED. NOR WERE THE PUNJAB LEADERS PERMITTED TO RECORD THEIR STATEMENTS. SO THE INDIAN NATIONAL CONGRESS SET UP AN UNOFFICIAL ENQUIRY COMMITTEE OF WHICH GANDHI WAS THE CHAIRMAN AND DAS ONE OF THE FOUR MEMBERS.

* THE BILL, AIMED AT SUPPRESSING THE NATIONAL MOVEMENT, EMPOWERED THE BRITISH GOVERNMENT TO DETAIN ANYONE WITHOUT A TRIAL.

BUT IT WAS ONLY DURING THE NAGPUR SESSION OF THE CONGRESS IN DECEMBER 1920 THAT DAS PLUNGED HEADLONG INTO THE MOVEMENT.

THE TIME HAS COME TO RESORT TO NON-CO-OPERATION IN EARNEST. I CALL ON LAWYERS TO BOYCOTT THE COURTS, ON STUDENTS TO BOYCOTT THEIR INSTITUTIONS, AND ON ALL MY COUNTRYMEN TO REFUSE TO PAY TAXES.

INDIAN NATIONAL CONGRESS

FOR THOSE STUDENTS WHO BOYCOTT COLLEGES, I SHALL INSTITUTE A NATIONAL COLLEGE. AS FOR MYSELF, I SHALL NO MORE PRACTISE LAW.

HE WAS AT THE PEAK OF HIS CAREER WHEN HE TOOK THIS OATH.

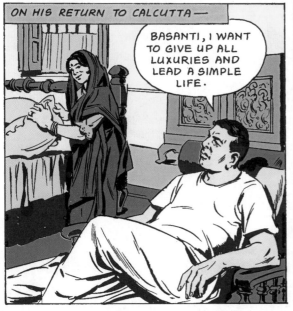

ON HIS RETURN TO CALCUTTA—

BASANTI, I WANT TO GIVE UP ALL LUXURIES AND LEAD A SIMPLE LIFE.

BASANTI SMILED.

ISN'T SMOKING THE HOOKAH A LUXURY?

IT IS!

CONTD. ON PAGE 19

THE STORY OF AMAR CHITRA KATHA

50 YEARS

AMAR CHITRA KATHA

A YEAR-LONG CELEBRATION OF FIVE DECADES OF STORYTELLING

WE PROUDLY PRESENT A SERIALISED RETELLING OF HOW OUR BELOVED FOUNDER, UNCLE PAI, FIRST STARTED AMAR CHITRA KATHA AND TINKLE!

LOOK OUT FOR A ONE-PAGE COMIC IN EVERY ISSUE THIS YEAR!

SARKAR! YOUR HOOKAH!

TAKE IT AWAY. I HAVE GIVEN UP TOBACCO. AND LISTEN...

...IF I SEE YOU AROUND I MAY BE TEMPTED TO SMOKE AGAIN. SO YOU MUST GO AWAY.

SARKAR, SHOULD I STARVE ON THE STREETS FOR NO FAULT OF MINE?

CERTAINLY NOT! NOT AFTER HAVING SERVED ME SO WELL! I SHALL GIVE YOU ENOUGH MONEY AND PROPERTY TO TAKE CARE OF YOUR NEEDS FOR THE REST OF YOUR LIFE.

THESE WESTERN CLOTHES MUST GO, TOO. I'LL MAKE A FINE BONFIRE OF THEM.

THE NEXT STEP HE TOOK WAS TO SIGN AWAY THE OWNERSHIP OF HIS MATERIAL WEALTH TO THE MOTHERLAND, REDUCING HIMSELF TO THE POSITION OF A MERE TRUSTEE.

AND THAT WAS WHEN A MEMBER OF THE BANGIYA SAHITYA PARISHAD CAME TO HIM.

I HAVE COME FOR A DONATION, SIR.

ALL THAT IS HERE NOW BELONGS TO THE MOTHERLAND.

THEN OUR LIBRARY COULD USE THESE BOOKS.

THEY ARE YOURS. MANY MORE WOULD HAVE ACCESS TO THEM IF THEY WERE IN YOUR LIBRARY.

THE NATION HENCEFORTH LOVINGLY REFERRED TO THE BRILLIANT, HUMANE BARRISTER-TURNED-SATYAGRAHI AS "DESHBANDHU" CHITTARANJAN DAS.

ONE DAY A STRANGER CAME TO SEE DESH-BANDHU.

MY FRIEND IN LONDON ASKED ME TO PERSONALLY DELIVER THIS LETTER TO YOU. HE COULD NOT RISK SENDING IT BY POST.

" I HAVE PASSED THE I.C.S. EXAMINATION BUT SERVICE UNDER AN ALIEN GOVERNMENT AND LOYALTY TO THE MOTHER-LAND DON'T GO HAND IN HAND. I WISH TO JOIN YOU", HE WRITES. GOOD! WE NEED YOUNG MEN LIKE HIM.

THE LETTER WAS FROM NONE OTHER THAN SUBHAS CHANDRA BOSE WHO WAS THEN IN LONDON.

MEANWHILE, A GROUP OF STUDENTS CAME TO MEET DESHBANDHU.

SIR, WE HAVE STARTED BOYCOTTING THEIR COLLEGES. WHEN WILL WE GET OUR NATIONAL COLLEGE ?

VERY SOON. I ASSURE YOU.

DESHBANDHU APPROACHED SEVERAL TRUSTS. MANY WERE RELUCTANT.

YOU WILL KINDLY EXCUSE US, DAS BABU. IT WOULD BE A FUTILE VENTURE. SUCH COLLEGES WILL NOT BE ALLOWED TO FUNCTION.

IN SPITE OF SUCH SCEPTICS DESHBANDHU STARTED THE GAURIYA SARVA VIDYAYATAN. MAHATMA GANDHI INAUGURATED THE COLLEGE AND SUBHAS CHANDRA BOSE WAS THE FIRST PRINCIPAL.

DESHBANDHU DESERVES OUR ADMIRATION FOR MAKING THIS DREAM COME TRUE WITHIN A MONTH OF OUR NAGPUR SESSION.

DESHBANDHU THEN BEGAN TO TOUR THE COUNTRY TO SPREAD THE MESSAGE OF THE CONGRESS. LARGE CROWDS GREETED HIM WHEREVER HE WENT.

WHAT WE WANT IS FREEDOM. NOT FOR THE ELITE ALONE, BUT FOR THE POOR TOO.

AT ONE STATION THE TRAIN HALTED AT 4 A.M. A SIKH ENTERED DESHBANDHU'S COMPARTMENT.

WHERE IS DESHBANDHU CHITTARAN-JAN DAS ?

HE IS SLEEPING. PLEASE DO NOT DISTURB HIM.

AH, THERE HE IS !

HEY WHAT IS THIS ! PUT ME DOWN !

NOW I AM HAPPY. I HAVE TRAVELLED FOR SEVEN DAYS ON FOOT JUST TO SEE YOU !

AND HUNDREDS OF PEOPLE LIKE ME ARE WAITING OUTSIDE TO PAY YOU THEIR RESPECTS.

DESHBANDHU KI JAI.

RAILWAY

THE PRINCE OF WALES WAS TO VISIT INDIA IN 1921 AND WAS TO REACH BOMBAY ON NOVEMBER 21 AND CALCUTTA ON DECEMBER 24.

I WANT VOLUNTEERS— A LAKH OF THEM. THEY WILL SELL KHADI IN THE STREETS AND TELL THE PEOPLE TO OBSERVE HARTAL DURING THE PRINCE'S VISIT.

HIS ONLY SON CHIRA RANJAN WAS ONE OF THE VOLUNTEERS. ANOTHER WAS HIS WIFE BASANTI DEVI.

WHAT ARE YOU DOING, MADAM?

I AM SELLING KHADI AND ASKING PEOPLE TO OBSERVE A HARTAL WHEN THE PRINCE OF WALES COMES TO CALCUTTA.

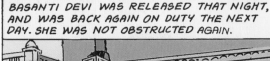

ONE OF THE FIRST TO BE TAKEN INTO CUSTODY WAS BASANTI DEVI.

YOU ARE UNDER ARREST! COME WITH ME.

WILLINGLY!

BASANTI DEVI WAS HELD IN HIGH ESTEEM AND MANY EVEN IN THE POLICE, PROTESTED.

MOTHER, TO ARREST YOU IS WRONG! I CANNOT TOLERATE IT ANY MORE. I SHALL RESIGN.

BASANTI DEVI WAS RELEASED THAT NIGHT, AND WAS BACK AGAIN ON DUTY THE NEXT DAY. SHE WAS NOT OBSTRUCTED AGAIN.

THE GOVERNOR OF BENGAL HAD A MEETING WITH DESHBANDHU.

I UNDERSTAND YOU ARE PLANNING ANOTHER INCIDENT WHEN THE PRINCE ARRIVES IN CALCUTTA ON 24TH DECEMBER. YOU MUST CALL IT OFF.

THAT IS AN ORDER OF THE CONGRESS. I HAVE NO AUTHORITY TO CALL IT OFF!

WELL, YOU COULD RESTRAIN THE VOLUNTEERS.

IMPOSSIBLE. THEY ARE BUT DISCHARGING THEIR DUTIES.

DAS KNEW HE WOULD SOON BE ARRESTED. BUT HE WAS NOT PERTURBED.

CHILD, COULD YOU SPREAD A MAT FOR ME ON THE FLOOR?

I WISH TO TRAIN MYSELF FOR PRISON LIFE.

AND DAS BEGAN TO SLEEP ON THE FLOOR.

TWO DAYS LATER —

THEY HAVE COME, FATHER.

I AM READY FOR THEM.

I WANT TO SEE THE WARRANT FOR MY ARREST.

IT IS NOT REQUIRED. YOU ARE ARRESTED UNDER SECTION 54.

WHEN WAS THE LAW CHANGED? SECTION 54 IS FOR CRIMINALS, NOT FOR POLITICAL WORKERS.

THE POLICE HAD NO ANSWER, BUT ARRESTED HIM NEVERTHELESS.

THE HEARING OF DESHBANDHU'S CASE WAS HELD INSIDE THE PRISON BECAUSE THE POLICE COULD NOT CONTROL THE CROWDS OUTSIDE THE COURT.

I SENTENCE YOU TO SIX MONTHS' SIMPLE IMPRISONMENT.

WILL YOU OPT FOR EUROPEAN CLASS, MR. DAS? YOU CAN GET FOOD FROM HOME.

WHAT IS GOOD ENOUGH FOR MY FELLOW PRISONERS IS GOOD ENOUGH FOR ME.

DESHBANDHU DAS WAS THE PRESIDENT-ELECT OF THE FORTHCOMING CONGRESS SESSION AT AHMEDABAD. SAROJINI NAIDU READ OUT THE SPEECH THAT HE WROTE IN PRISON.

...IT WOULD BE SHEER HYPOCRISY ON OUR PART TO EXTEND A NATIONAL WELCOME TO THE AMBASSADOR OF THE POWER THAT WOULD DENY US OUR ELEMENTARY RIGHTS...

SUBHAS BOSE AND MANY OTHER FOLLOWERS OF DESHBANDHU WERE ALSO IN PRISON AT THE SAME TIME. THEY HAD LONG DISCUSSIONS.

I HAVE ALWAYS ADMIRED YOU. BUT AFTER BEING NEAR YOU AND KNOWING YOUR INNERMOST THOUGHTS I ADMIRE YOU ALL THE MORE.

DESHBANDHU'S HEALTH BEGAN TO DECLINE IN PRISON. ONE DAY —

BABU, YOU NEED SOMEBODY TO LOOK AFTER YOU. I WANT TO BE OF SERVICE.

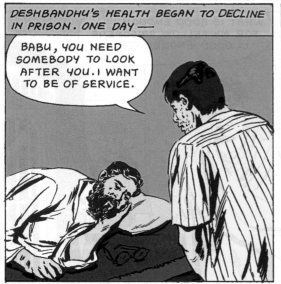

WHO ARE YOU? WHAT IS YOUR NAME?

MATHOOR, BABU. I AM ONLY A COMMON THIEF.

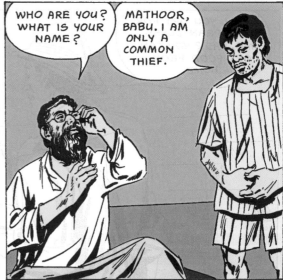

THROUGHOUT DESHBANDHU'S ILLNESS MATHOOR WAITED ON HIM AND ATTENDED TO HIS NEEDS.

WHEN DESHBANDHU WAS TO BE RELEASED—

BABU, WHEN YOU LEAVE I WILL BE LIKE AN ORPHAN!

YOU TOO WILL BE RELEASED SOON! DO COME AND MEET ME.

WHEN MATHOOR WAS RELEASED, THERE WAS SOMEONE WAITING FOR HIM, OUTSIDE THE PRISON GATE.

ARE YOU MATHOOR? COME WITH ME. CHITTARANJAN BABU HAS SENT FOR YOU.

MATHOOR, WOULD YOU LIKE TO SERVE IN MY HOUSE?

ME? IN YOUR HOUSE? WHO COULD ASK FOR MORE! AM I DREAMING?

THE HOUSEHOLD DID NOT APPROVE OF DAS'S GESTURE.

HOW CAN YOU BE SO TRUSTING TOWARDS A THIEF?

MATHOOR IS A CRIMINAL.

WAS, MY DEAR. I KNOW MATHOOR WELL. HAVE NO FEAR!

THE GAYA SESSION OF THE CONGRESS IN DECEMBER 1922 WITNESSED A SPLIT IN THE PARTY. DAS, AS ELECTED PRESIDENT, MADE A SPEECH.

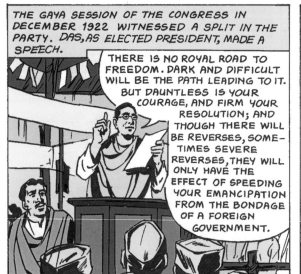

THERE IS NO ROYAL ROAD TO FREEDOM. DARK AND DIFFICULT WILL BE THE PATH LEADING TO IT. BUT DAUNTLESS IS YOUR COURAGE, AND FIRM YOUR RESOLUTION; AND THOUGH THERE WILL BE REVERSES, SOMETIMES SEVERE REVERSES, THEY WILL ONLY HAVE THE EFFECT OF SPEEDING YOUR EMANCIPATION FROM THE BONDAGE OF A FOREIGN GOVERNMENT.

HE MOVED A RESOLUTION SUPPORTING COUNCIL ENTRY. IT WAS DEFEATED. MOTILAL AND DESHBANDHU RESIGNED FROM THE WORKING COMMITTEE.

OUR DIFFERENCE WILL ONLY BE FOR A SHORT WHILE. THE MAJORITY WILL SOON ACCEPT OUR POINT OF VIEW.

WITHIN THE CONGRESS, DAS AND MOTILAL NEHRU FORMED THE SWARAJYA PARTY.

DESHBANDHU TOURED ALL OVER INDIA TO EXPLAIN THE SWARAJYA PARTY'S PROGRAMME.

IF WE BOYCOTT THE LEGISLATURE THE GOVERNMENT WILL BE HAPPY. FOR SUCH A STEP WOULD MAKE ITS WORK THAT MUCH SIMPLER.

WE WILL TAKE THE NON-CO-OPERATION MOVEMENT TO THE LEGISLATURE. WE WILL EFFECTIVELY BLOCK ALL GOVERNMENT MEASURES AS MEMBERS OF THE LEGISLATURE.

DESHBANDHU MUSTERED A GOOD DEAL OF SUPPORT, AND AT THE 1923 SESSION OF THE CONGRESS IN DELHI THE MOOD WAS DIFFERENT.

IT IS USELESS TO BOYCOTT LEGISLATURES. WE SHOULD WIN AS MANY SEATS AS POSSIBLE. THE CONGRESS WILL NOT COME IN THE WAY OF THE SWARAJISTS.

DESHBANDHU AND HIS MEN CONTESTED THE ELECTION.

IT'S A LANDSLIDE VICTORY!

DESHBANDHU KI JAI!

THE GOVERNOR INVITED DESHBANDHU TO FORM A MINISTRY.

THIS IS MY REPLY. "MEMBERS OF MY PARTY ARE PLEDGED TO PUT AN END TO THE PRESENT GOVERNMENT. I DECLINE TO ACCEPT YOUR EXCELLENCY'S GRACIOUS OFFER".

THE SWARAJYA PARTY ACTED AS A POWERFUL OPPOSITION IN THE BENGAL LEGISLATIVE COUNCIL AND VOTED DOWN ALL UNPOPULAR MEASURES.

THIS IS THE THIRD TIME WE HAVE DEFEATED THE OFFICIAL RESOLUTION. THE GOVERNMENT JUST CAN'T FUNCTION!

I KNEW NON-CO-OPERATION WOULD BE VERY EFFECTIVE!

ELECTIONS TO THE CALCUTTA CORPORATION WERE HELD AND HERE TOO DESHBANDHU AND HIS MEN WON EASILY. DESHBANDHU WAS ELECTED MAYOR AND SUBHAS CHANDRA BOSE BECAME HIS CHIEF EXECUTIVE OFFICER.

WE INDIANS REGARD THE POOR AS GOD! I SHALL TRY TO DIRECT THE ACTIVITIES OF THE CORPORATION TO SERVING THE POOR.

THE PRESSURE OF CEASELESS WORK BEGAN TO TELL ON DESHBANDHU'S HEALTH.

YOU MUST GO TO THE HILLS FOR A CHANGE. WE WILL MANAGE HERE. DON'T WORRY ABOUT US.

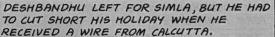

DESHBANDHU LEFT FOR SIMLA, BUT HE HAD TO CUT SHORT HIS HOLIDAY WHEN HE RECEIVED A WIRE FROM CALCUTTA.

THEY HAVE ARRESTED SUBHAS. I WILL HAVE TO RUSH DOWN.

MEETINGS WERE HELD IN PROTEST. DESHBANDHU SPOKE AT THE CALCUTTA CORPORATION.

IF LOVE FOR ONE'S COUNTRY IS A CRIME, SUBHAS IS A CRIMINAL. SO AM I! WHY WAS HE ARRESTED? THERE IS NO EXPLANATION. IS THIS LAW?

MAHATMA GANDHI CAME TO CALCUTTA AND NOW THERE WAS COMPLETE RAPPORT BETWEEN HIM AND DESHBANDHU.

YOU WERE RIGHT! IF THE BUREAUCRACY HAS TO USE SUCH MEASURES TO REPRESS ITS ELECTED REPRESENTATIVES, NON-CO-OPERATION HAS SUCCEEDED!

THIS RAPPORT WAS CONFIRMED AT THE BELGAUM CONFERENCE HELD IN 1924.

BOYCOTT OF FOREIGN CLOTH WILL REMAIN BUT BOYCOTT OF LEGISLATURES IS HENCEFORTH WITHDRAWN. THE CONGRESS WILL ADOPT THE PROGRAMME OF THE SWARAJYA PARTY.

THIS WAS A VICTORY FOR THE STAND TAKEN BY DAS AND MOTILAL.

DESHBANDHU'S HEALTH DETERIORATED.

DESHBANDHU, YOUR HEALTH WILL IMPROVE ONLY IF YOU HAVE A CHANGE OF AIR. COME TO DARJEELING AS MY GUEST.

THE SPEAKER WAS AN OLD FRIEND AND COLLEAGUE, SHRI N.N.SIRCAR.

BASANTI, LET US GO TO DARJEELING. SIRCAR WILL NOT TAKE NO FOR AN ANSWER.

GANDHI HAPPENED TO BE IN BENGAL AND JOINED DESHBANDHU AT DARJEELING. THEY WENT FOR WALKS AND HELD LENGTHY DISCUSSIONS.

THE HOUSE HAD BECOME A SPINNING CLASS!

I CAN NEVER SPIN ON THE CHARKHA, WITHOUT BASANTI'S HELP, BAPUJI. SHE HOLDS THE KEY TO MY PLYING THE CHARKHA.

IT'S JUST A FEMININE WILE TO MAKE HER HUSBAND DEPENDENT ON HER.

THE HOST HAD ARRANGED FOR FIVE GOATS AS GANDHI DRANK ONLY GOAT'S MILK.

DO THEY GIVE MILK PROPERLY?

NO, SIR. OF THESE FIVE, ONLY TWO GIVE MILK. THE OTHER THREE JUST REFUSE.

THESE THREE HAVE TAKEN TO NON-CO-OPERATION! PUT THEM IN A JAIL. THE LOYAL ONES SHOULD GET TITLES FROM BAPU!

DESHBANDHU'S FEVER USED TO COME OFF AND ON.

THIS REMINDS ME OF OLD TIMES. KASTURBA USED TO SIT AT MY FEET AS I NOW SIT HERE!

A SHORT WHILE AFTER GANDHI LEFT, DESHBANDHU HAD A SERVE RELAPSE.

YOUR PULSE IS STEADILY GETTING FEEBLER. LET ME CALL ANOTHER DOCTOR.

NO! LET THERE BE NO CHANGE IN DOCTORS NOW.

VERY SOON, IT WAS OVER. THE FIFTY-FOUR-YEAR OLD STALWART OF THE FREEDOM STRUGGLE PASSED AWAY. THE COUNTRY WAS PLUNGED INTO GLOOM. HALF A MILLION PEOPLE ACCOMPANIED THE BIER THROUGH THE STREETS OF CALCUTTA.

AT THE CONDOLENCE MEETING GANDHI WAS THE ONLY SPEAKER.

DESHBANDHU IS NO MORE. BUT HIS NAME WILL REMAIN IMMORTAL. HIS SERVICE AND SACRIFICE WERE MATCHLESS. MAY HIS EXAMPLE INSPIRE US TO NOBLER EFFORT.

HIS LIFE DID INSPIRE THE PEOPLE TO CARRY ON THE STRUGGLE...

...WHICH CONTRIBUTED IN NO SMALL MEASURE TO INDIA WINNING HER INDEPENDENCE ON AUGUST 15, 1947.

RASH BEHARI BOSE

INDEPENDENT INDIA WAS HIS LIFE-LONG DREAM

The route to your roots

RASH BEHARI BOSE

As a schoolboy and a young man he rebelled against the unfair accusation that the people of Bengal lacked courage. Determined to prove otherwise Rash Behari Bose worked to free India from British rule for 40 years. Wanted by the British police his life was one of escapades and adventure. The Indian National Army that he founded grew into a formidable force of 40,000 soldiers. He was rightly called the Father of the Indian Independence Movement in East Asia.

Script
Prof.Satyavrata Ghosh
And
Luis Fernandes

Illustrations
Souren Roy

Editor
Anant Pai

Cover illustration by: C.M. Vitankar

RASH BEHARI BOSE

AT THE TURN OF THE CENTURY, A BOY IN THE NINTH STANDARD OF DUPLEIX SCHOOL AT CHANDERNAGORE, SAT THROUGH HIS HISTORY CLASS RESENTING EVERY WORD HIS TEACHER UTTERED.

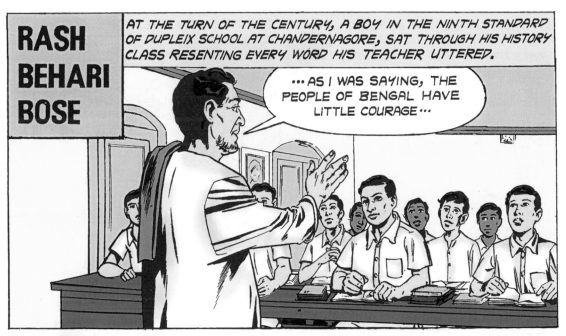

...AS I WAS SAYING, THE PEOPLE OF BENGAL HAVE LITTLE COURAGE...

...THAT WAS WHY BAKTIAR KHILJI COULD CONQUER BENGAL WITH ONLY SEVENTEEN CAVALRYMEN...

THAT'S NOT CORRECT, SIR.

HE HAD MANY MORE MEN THAN THAT! BESIDES...

ARE YOU TRYING TO TEACH ME HISTORY?

I AM JUST TELLING YOU THE FACTS...

GET OUT OF MY CLASS YOU IMPERTINENT BOY!

AND I'LL SEE THAT YOU'RE KEPT OUT FOR GOOD.

THE BOY'S NAME WAS RASH BEHARI BOSE. HIS HISTORY TEACHER SAW TO IT THAT HE WAS EXPELLED FROM THE SCHOOL.

SOMETIME LATER, THE BOY RAN AWAY FROM HOME···

···AND TRIED TO JOIN THE ARMY. BUT—

SORRY, WE DON'T TAKE BENGALIS. YOU PEOPLE CAN'T FIGHT.

CAN'T FIGHT?

CAN'T FIGHT! I'LL SHOW THESE BRITISHERS.

I'LL JOIN THEIR ARMY SOMEHOW, LEARN THEIR TECHNIQUE AND THEN···

···AND THEN I'LL USE IT TO DRIVE THEM OUT OF MY COUNTRY!

HE WENT TO FORT WILLIAM IN CALCUTTA, TO TRY FOR A JOB THERE.

YOUR NAME?

RASH BEHARI.

HE GOT A JOB.

BEING A CLERK ISN'T THE SAME AS BEING A SOLDIER BUT IT WILL HELP ME LEARN A LOT ABOUT THE ARMY.

A FEW WEEKS LATER HE WAS SUMMONED BY THE COMMANDING OFFICER.

WHAT IS YOUR FULL NAME?

RASH BEHARI.

YOUR FULL NAME IS RASH BEHARI BOSE, ISN'T IT?

YES.

YOU KNOW WE DON'T CARE FOR BENGALIS HERE, DON'T YOU?

I KNOW, SIR. THAT'S WHY...

SHUT UP! AND GET OUT!

RASH BEHARI STRODE OUT WITHOUT ANOTHER WORD.

THEY HAVE NOT HEARD THE LAST OF ME YET.

RASH BEHARI WENT TO DEHRA DUN AND FOUND HIMSELF A JOB IN THE CHEMISTRY DEPARTMENT OF THE FOREST RESEARCH INSTITUTE. FROM THERE HE SMUGGLED OUT CHEMICALS IN FLOWER-POTS···

···AND IN HIS SPARE TIME TAUGHT HIMSELF HOW TO MAKE BOMBS···

···AND USE FIREARMS.

GRADUALLY, HE BEGAN TO TRAIN OTHER YOUNG MEN TOO. RASH BEHARI WAS DETERMINED TO SHOW THAT BENGALIS COULD BE COURAGEOUS FIGHTERS EVEN AGAINST THE MIGHTY BRITISH.

SEVEN YEARS LATER, ON DECEMBER 23, 1912, LORD HARDINGE, VICEROY OF INDIA, WAS PASSING THROUGH CHANDNI CHOWK IN DELHI.

THE PROCESSION WAS AN AWESOME SPECTACLE, REFLECTING THE MIGHT AND GLORY OF THE BRITISH EMPIRE.

RAJAHS AND NAWABS FLANKED THE DIGNITARY. GUNS BOOMED IN SALUTE. AND ABOVE THEM ALL FLUTTERED THE UNION JACK.

SUDDENLY—

BOOM!

MY GOD!
THE VICEROY IS
KILLED!

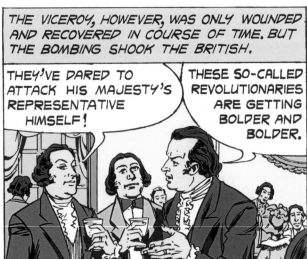

THE VICEROY, HOWEVER, WAS ONLY WOUNDED AND RECOVERED IN COURSE OF TIME. BUT THE BOMBING SHOOK THE BRITISH.

THEY'VE DARED TO ATTACK HIS MAJESTY'S REPRESENTATIVE HIMSELF!

THESE SO-CALLED REVOLUTIONARIES ARE GETTING BOLDER AND BOLDER.

THE CULPRIT MUST BE CAUGHT AND HANGED!

THE POLICE AND BRITISH INTELLIGENCE UNITS SWUNG INTO ACTION. SEVERAL WEEKS LATER—

WE'VE GOT ALL THE GUILTY ONES, SIR··· ALL EXCEPT ONE.

OH?

WHO IS THIS ONE WHO GOT AWAY?

A BENGALI···
RASH BEHARI BOSE.

HE IS TWENTY-EIGHT YEARS OLD. WE SUSPECT THAT HE PLOTTED THE WHOLE THING.

UNFORTUNATELY WE DON'T HAVE THE FAINTEST IDEA WHERE HE IS.

BUT IF THE POLICE DID NOT KNOW WHERE TO LOOK FOR RASH BEHARI BOSE, INDIAN REVOLUTIONARIES DID.

KNOCK KNOCK!

STAY OUT OF SIGHT, DADA. I'LL SEE WHO IT IS.

YES?

I AM VISHNU GANESH PINGLEY. I HAVE COME TO MEET NARENDRA-NATH SEN.

THERE IS NO ONE HERE BY THAT NAME. WHO HAS SENT YOU?

JATIN DADA.

I HAVE A LETTER FROM JATIN DADA. BUT I CAN'T GIVE IT TO ANYONE EXCEPT SEN.

ALL RIGHT, COME IN.

*FIRST WORLD WAR

BUT WE MUST FIRST FIND OUT WHETHER THE GHADR MEN ARE READY.

LEAVE THAT TO ME.

SACHIN TOURED THE PUNJAB AND CAME BACK WITH AN ENCOURAGING REPORT.

THEIR MORALE IS HIGH, DADA. THEY ARE ALL WELL-ARMED.

THEY HAVE GUNS, AMMUNITION AND BOMBS; AND THEY ARE IMPATIENT FOR ACTION.

THEN WE SHOULD NOT DENY IT TO THEM.

BUT I HAVE BEEN THINKING, SACHIN. BRITAIN HAS ONLY 30,000 SOLDIERS IN INDIA AND MOST OF THEM ARE INDIANS.

WHY NOT GET THEM ON TO OUR SIDE?

THAT'S A GOOD IDEA!

I'LL MAKE A TOUR OF THE CANTONMENTS. I'M SURE THE INDIAN SOLDIERS WOULD LIKE TO THROW IN THEIR LOT WITH US.

RASH BEHARI VISITED SEVERAL CANTONMENTS DISGUISED AS AN ARMY OFFICER. THE RESPONSE WAS IMMEDIATE AND ENTHUSIASTIC.

THIS IS A FINE OPPORTUNITY TO THROW OFF FOREIGN RULE ONCE AND FOR ALL··· LET US RISE TO THE OCCASION!

WE ARE WITH YOU.

RASH BEHARI AND HIS COMRADES PLANNED A MASS UPRISING IN THE NORTH-EAST ON FEBRUARY 21, 1915.

TWENTY-SIX CANTONMENTS ARE PREPARING TO REVOLT.

THE SOLDIERS HAVE BEEN INSTRUCTED TO CAPTURE THEIR ENGLISH OFFICERS AND TO LOOT THE TREASURIES. THE GHADR MEN WILL LAUNCH A SIMULTANEOUS ATTACK.

THE BENGALIS WILL JOIN THE REBELLION WHEN THE ARMS FROM GERMANY ARRIVE. THE ARMS WILL BE OFF-LOADED IN BENGAL.

EMISSARIES HAVE BEEN SENT TO BURMA AND SINGAPORE TOO. ALL ASIA IS PREPARING TO THROW OFF THE SHACKLES OF IMPERIALISM.

IT WAS DECIDED THAT RASH BEHARI SHOULD CONDUCT THE OPERATION FROM LAHORE. SO HE, PINGLEY AND SACHIN WENT TO LAHORE AND FOUND A SUITABLE HOUSE FROM WHICH HE COULD OPERATE.

MEANWHILE THE BRITISH INTELLIGENCE WAS TRYING TO DISCOVER WHAT THE REVOLUTIONARIES WERE UP TO. FINALLY—

WE'VE MADE CONTACT WITH ONE OF THEM, SIR, A FELLOW NAMED KIRPAL SINGH.

GOOD!

HE HAS AGREED TO MEET ONE OF MY MEN AT THE RAILWAY STATION TODAY.

WHEN KIRPAL SINGH WENT TO HIS RENDEZVOUS, HE WAS SEEN BY ONE OF HIS COMRADES.

WHAT'S HE DOING HERE? HE'S SUPPOSED TO BE AT MIANWALI.

THE MAN IMMEDIATELY REPORTED TO RASH BEHARI.

SO WE HAD A TRAITOR IN OUR MIDST.

WE'D BETTER CALL THE WHOLE THING OFF.

NO!

CRASH!

YOU'RE UNDER ARREST!

AS THE REVOLUTIONARIES WERE BEING LED AWAY—

SALAM, SAAB!

NOBODY PAID ANY ATTENTION TO THE MAN CARRYING AWAY THE NIGHT SOIL.

BUT HE WAS NONE OTHER THAN RASH BEHARI BOSE.

THE POLICE CAPTURED SEVERAL PROMINENT REVOLUTIONARIES IN THE RAID. BUT BOSE HAD GOT AWAY.

THIS ANNOYED THE BRITISH. THEY CORDONED OFF LAHORE AND ORGANISED A SEARCH FOR HIM.

BUT HE PROVED TOO ELUSIVE FOR THEM. DRESSED AS A PATHAN, HE AND PINGLEY WHO TOO HAD ESCAPED CALMLY BOARDED A TRAIN...

...AND LEFT THE CITY FOR VARANASI.

PINGLEY, HOWEVER, GOT OFF AT MEERUT. SOME TIME LATER HE WAS BETRAYED BY ONE OF HIS COLLEAGUES AND HE WAS CAUGHT AND HANGED.

RASH BEHARI WAS IN VARANASI FOR A MONTH. WHEN THE POLICE STARTED CLOSING IN ON HIM, HE DISGUISED HIMSELF AS A PUJARI AND FLED TO CHANDERNAGORE, HIS NATIVE PLACE. IN CHANDERNAGORE AS HE WAS WALKING ON THE STREET—

A POLICEMAN!

HE'S COMING TOWARDS ME! SHOULD I RUN?

BUT TO HIS ASTONISHMENT —

WHEW! THAT WAS A NARROW ESCAPE!

IN CHANDERNAGORE, HE MET SACHIN AND OTHER LEADERS WHO HAD MANAGED TO EVADE THE POLICE.

DADA, THE POLICE ARE MOVING HEAVEN AND EARTH TO CATCH YOU.

YOUR PICTURE IS UP ON POSTERS EVERYWHERE. BRITISH SPIES ARE WORKING DAY AND NIGHT.

IT WOULD BE A GREAT BLOW TO THE FREEDOM MOVEMENT IF YOU WERE CAUGHT. YOU MUST FLEE THE COUNTRY.

WHERE CAN I GO?

WE ARE LOOKING FOR THIS MAN, CAPTAIN. HIS NAME IS RASH BEHARI BOSE.

I HAVEN'T SEEN HIM. YOU MAY SEARCH THE SHIP IF YOU WISH.

THE POLICE SEARCHED THE SHIP THOROUGHLY...

...BUT RASH BEHARI'S DISGUISE WAS PERFECT.

AS I WAS SAYING, THE WEATHER...

HE'S NOT ON BOARD, SIR.

SORRY. WE HAVE BEEN MISINFORMED.

AS THE SHIP LEFT THE SHORE—

THIS IS MY MOTHERLAND, I AM LEAVING BEHIND... I STAKED MY LIFE... FOR HER LIBERATION AND I SHALL DO SO IN THE FUTURE...

S.S. SANUKI

RASH BEHARI WAS NEVER TO SEE HIS BELOVED COUNTRY AGAIN.

HE LANDED IN JAPAN ON JUNE 15.

SOMETIME LATER HE MET BHAGWAN SINGH, ANOTHER REVOLUTIONARY.

BHAGWAN SINGH PUT HIM IN TOUCH WITH THE GERMAN CONSULATE IN SHANGHAI* AT THE CONSULATE—

I NEED GUNS AND AMMUNITION TO SEND BACK HOME.

WE'LL SEE WHAT WE CAN DO.

A GERMAN AGENT NAMED NIELSEN HELPED HIM TO GET ARMS···

···BUT THE FIRST CONSIGNMENT RASH BEHARI DESPATCHED TO INDIA WAS SEIZED BY THE BRITISH.

AFTER THAT HE SENT TWO SHIPLOADS OF ARMS AND AMMUNITION. BUT THESE SHIPS TOO WERE INTERCEPTED BY THE BRITISH.

* A CHINESE CITY

AS HE CONTINUED HIS EFFORTS TO SEND ARMS TO INDIA, HE BEGAN TO MAKE HIS PRESENCE FELT IN JAPAN. ON NOVEMBER 15, 1915, ALONG WITH LALA LAJPATRAI HE ORGANISED A POLITICAL MEETING IN TOKYO. THE LALA LASHED OUT AT THE BRITISH.

LADIES AND GENTLEMEN, WE OF THE ANCIENT LAND OF INDIA MEET IN THE LAND OF THE RISING SUN TO TELL THE WORLD ABOUT THE CRUELTY AND INJUSTICE OF BRITISH RULE IN THE EAST...

AND WHEN HIS TURN CAME TO SPEAK, RASH BEHARI DID NOT RESTRAIN HIMSELF EITHER.

...WE HAVE SUFFERED LONG ENOUGH AT THE HANDS OF THE IMPERIALISTS. LET THERE NOW BE AN END...

THE BRITISH GOVERNMENT WAS ALARMED. IT PERSUADED JAPAN TO ISSUE AN EXTRADITION WARRANT AGAINST THE TWO INDIANS.

LALA LAJPATRAI FLED TO AMERICA. RASH BEHARI BOSE WENT INTO HIDING.

ONCE AGAIN HE BECAME A HUNTED MAN. THEN ONE DAY AS THE POLICE WERE CLOSING IN ON HIM—

GET IN.

WHO ARE YOU?

A FRIEND.

SOMA, YOU WILL TAKE CHARGE OF THIS YOUNG MAN. AS TRUE SAMURAI, IT IS OUR DUTY TO SAVE MEN IN DISTRESS.

OH!

THE POLICE ARE WAITING FOR YOU AT THE FRONT GATE. BUT DON'T WORRY. WE'LL GET YOU OUT OF HERE.

A LITTLE LATER, WEARING JAPANESE CLOTHES, RASH BEHARI WALKED OUT OF DR. TOYOMA'S HOUSE THROUGH THE BACK DOOR.

HE ENTERED THE NEIGHBOURING MANSION...

...AND LEFT THAT HOUSE TOO THE SAME WAY. SOMA WAS WAITING FOR HIM THERE WITH A CAR.

OUTSIDE DR. TOYOMA'S FRONT GATE—

I THOUGHT I HEARD A CAR STARTING.

DON'T WORRY. OUR MAN IS STILL INSIDE.

CAN'T YOU SEE HIS SHOES OUTSIDE THE DOOR?

THE JAPANESE POLICE, LIKE THEIR BRITISH COUNTERPARTS, WERE SOON TO REALISE THAT RASH BEHARI WAS NOT AN EASY MAN TO CATCH.

EVEN BEFORE IT DAWNED ON THE POLICEMEN OUTSIDE DR. TOYOMA'S HOUSE THAT THEY HAD BEEN FOOLED, RASH BEHARI HAD ALIGHTED IN FRONT OF A BAKERY OWNED BY MR. SOMA.

NAKAMURAYA

THIS IS MY WIFE.

WE HAVE TO HIDE MR. BOSE. HE IS UNDER ORDERS OF DEPORTATION.

OH!

IF HE IS DEPORTED, THE BRITISH WILL HANG HIM.

THAT WOULD BE TERRIBLE.

LET US HIDE HIM IN THE ATTIC.

RASH BEHARI SPENT FOUR MONTHS WITH SOMA. THEN ONE DAY —

THE DEPORTATION ORDER AGAINST YOU HAS BEEN WITHDRAWN.

AT LAST!

NOW I CAN GET BACK TO MY WORK. I CAN NEVER THANK YOU ENOUGH FOR YOUR HELP.

BUT THE REVOLUTIONARY'S TROUBLES WERE NOT OVER. THE BRITISH AGENTS BEGAN TO DOG HIM HOPING TO KIDNAP HIM···

···OR TO SILENCE HIM FOREVER.

24

IN *1918,* HE MARRIED MISS TOSHIKO SOMA, THE DAUGHTER OF THE MAN WHO HAD GIVEN HIM SHELTER WHEN HE WAS HIDING FROM THE POLICE. DR. TOYOMA CONDUCTED THE CEREMONY.

LIFE WAS NOT EASY FOR THE COUPLE. THEY HAD TO CHANGE HOUSES EVERY FEW WEEKS TO THROW THE SPIES FOLLOWING THEM OFF THE SCENT.

I AM SORRY YOU HAVE TO GO THROUGH SO MUCH HARDSHIP FOR MY SAKE.

EVERYTHING WILL BE FINE ONCE YOU GET YOUR JAPANESE CITIZENSHIP.

FINALLY, IN *1923—*

TOSHIKO, THE GOVERNMENT HAS GRANTED ME JAPANESE CITIZENSHIP!

THE BRITISH DARE NOT TOUCH ME NOW. WE NEED NOT HIDE ANY LONGER.

TOSHIKO, HOWEVER, WAS WORN OUT BY THE TENSIONS AND HARDSHIPS SHE HAD TO SUFFER DURING THEIR YEARS OF HIDING. SHE DIED TWO YEARS LATER, LEAVING BEHIND TWO CHILDREN.

RASH BEHARI ENTERED JAPANESE PUBLIC LIFE. HE HAD MASTERED JAPANESE IN THE FIRST FEW MONTHS OF HIS STAY IN JAPAN AND NOW HE BEGAN TO ADDRESS MEETINGS, GIVE LECTURES AND WRITE ARTICLES IN THAT LANGUAGE. THE JAPANESE BEGAN TO CALL HIM 'SENSEI' OR TEACHER.

HIS THEME WAS INVARIABLY THE SAME. THE ONENESS OF THE ASIAN PEOPLE.

ALL ASIANS SHOULD UNITE TO FIGHT BRITISH IMPERIALISM···!

IN 1924, HE FOUNDED THE INDIAN INDEPENDENCE LEAGUE. THE PURPOSE OF THE LEAGUE WAS TO PROMOTE THE CAUSE OF INDIAN INDEPENDENCE.

HE WAS STILL CARRYING ON THE FIGHT SEVENTEEN YEARS LATER WHEN JAPAN ENTERED THE SECOND WORLD WAR ON THE SIDE OF GERMANY.

THE JAPANESE ARMY SWEPT ACROSS SOUTHEAST ASIA.

BANZAI*!

THIS WAS THE OPPORTUNITY RASH BEHARI WAS WAITING FOR. HE APPROACHED THE JAPANESE ARMY AUTHORITIES.

JAPAN AND INDIA NOW HAVE A COMMON ENEMY— BRITAIN.

GIVE ME PERMISSION TO ORGANISE INDIANS IN EAST ASIA INTO AN ANTI-BRITISH ARMY.

YOU MAY GO AHEAD.

OUR GOALS ARE THE SAME. LET US WORK TOGETHER.

BEFORE SETTING OUT ON THE GREAT ADVENTURE, HE WENT TO SEE HIS OLD FRIEND, DR. TOYOMA, WHO WAS ON HIS DEATH-BED.

SENSEI, THE TIME HAS COME AT LAST···INDEPENDENCE FOR INDIA WAS A DREAM FOR A LONG TIME···

*A JAPANESE WAR CRY

...BUT IT IS TO BE A REALITY NOW. I AM EIGHTY-EIGHT BUT I WOULD LIKE TO SEE YOU SUCCEED BEFORE I PASS AWAY.

YOUR BLESSINGS ARE MY STRONGEST WEAPONS.

HE SOUGHT THE BLESSINGS OF TOSHIKO'S PARENTS TOO.

MOTHER, I HAVE DEVOTED ALL MY LIFE TO THE CAUSE OF INDIAN INDEPENDENCE. THE TIME HAS NOW COME FOR THE FINAL ONSLAUGHT.

GOODBYE, MY DEAREST ONES.

RASH BEHARI HOPED TO ORGANISE INDIANS IN EAST ASIA INTO A STRONG ARMY WHICH COULD MARCH INTO INDIA AND OVERTHROW THE GOVERNMENT THERE.

AND GRADUALLY HIS EFFORTS IN THIS DIRECTION BEGAN TO BEAR FRUIT. HE WAS THE CENTRAL FIGURE AT THE NOW FAMOUS BANGKOK CONFERENCE OF 1942 WHEN INDIAN LEADERS FROM ALL OVER ASIA MET TO CHALK OUT A PLAN OF ACTION TO LIBERATE THEIR HOMELAND.

UNITY, FAITH AND SACRIFICE OUR MOTTO.

AT THE BANGKOK CONFERENCE, THE INDIAN INDEPENDENCE LEAGUE WAS REORGANISED AND ITS MILITARY WING WAS NAMED THE **INDIAN NATIONAL ARMY** (INA). RASH BEHARI WAS APPOINTED PRESIDENT OF BOTH THE IIL AND THE INA.

THE **INA** COMMANDED BY CAPTAIN MOHAN SINGH ULTIMATELY GREW TO A FORCE OF FORTY THOUSAND MEN.

AS THIS ARMY PREPARED FOR ITS ROLE, RASH BEHARI WENT ON THE AIR TO EXHORT HIS COUNTRYMEN BACK HOME TO ACTION.

COMPATRIOTS AT HOME, YOU HAVE DECLARED WAR ON BRITAIN. AND THE BRITISH HAVE DRAWN FIRST BLOOD... THE ARREST OF OUR GREAT LEADERS IS ONLY THE BEGINNING. BRITAIN IS AT BAY. THE BRITISH WILL FORCE A BLOODBATH ON YOU...

ON JANUARY 26, 1943, HE REMINDED HIS COUNTRYMEN OF THE HISTORIC IMPORTANCE OF INDEPENDENCE DAY, AGAIN IN A BROADCAST.

···ON JANUARY 26, 1930, THE INDIAN NATION UNFURLED THE BANNER OF ANTI-BRITISH REVOLUTION. INDIA STANDS ON THE THRESHOLD OF COMPLETE INDEPENDENCE TODAY— THE ANNIVERSARY OF OUR GRIM RESOLVE. VANDE MATARAM!

BUT NOW THE GREAT FIGHTER WAS SLOWING DOWN DUE TO OLD AGE.

MY BELOVED COUNTRY WILL SOON BECOME FREE. BUT A YOUNGER MAN MUST CARRY ON THE STRUGGLE NOW.

FINALLY ON JULY 4, 1943, AT A MAMMOTH MEETING AT SINGAPORE —

FRIENDS AND COMRADES IN ARMS, IN YOUR PRESENCE TODAY I RESIGN MY OFFICE AND APPOINT DESHASEVAK SUBHAS CHANDRA BOSE PRESIDENT OF THE INDIAN INDEPENDENCE LEAGUE···INDIA'S BEST IS REPRESENTED IN HIM···

RASH BEHARI BOSE DIED ON JANUARY 29, 1945. PAYING TRIBUTE TO HIM SUBHAS CHANDRA BOSE SAID, "HE WAS THE FATHER OF THE INDIAN INDEPENDENCE MOVEMENT IN EAST ASIA···"

Amar Chitra Katha's

EPICS & MYTHOLOGY

BRAVEHEARTS

VISIONARIES

FABLES & HUMOUR

INDIAN CLASSICS

CONTEMPORARY CLASSICS

EXCITING STORY CATEGORIES, ONE AMAZING DESTINATION.

From the episodes of Mahabharata to the wit of Birbal,
from the valour of Shivaji to the teachings of Tagore,
from the adventures of Pratapan to the tales of Ruskin Bond –
Amar Chitra Katha stories span across different genres to get you the best of literature.

A NATION AWAKES

THE MARCH TO FREEDOM

The route to your roots

A NATION AWAKES

When Lord Curzon partitioned Bengal with the intention of weakening the people, it only served to unite them and strengthen their desire for freedom. The weapon they chose was 'Swadeshi' and the blow was aimed at European business interests. The movement spread and the cry 'Vande Mataram' resounded throughout the land. The movement caused a split in the National Congress. The moderates, who believed in continuing with petitions to the government, parted ways with the extremists who believed in agitating for their rights. The period saw a spurt in revolutionary activities. Despite all differences the people continued the struggle till the partition of Bengal was annulled.

Script	Illustrations	Editor
Subba Rao	Ram Waeerkar	Anant Pai

A NATION AWAKES

AT THE BEGINNING OF THE TWENTIETH CENTURY BENGAL PRESENTED A PICTURE OF UNITY IN DIVERSITY. RICH AND POOR, EDUCATED AND UNEDUCATED, BROAD-MINDED AND NARROW-MINDED BELONGING TO BOTH HINDU AND MUSLIM COMMUNITIES WOULD SINK THEIR DIFFERENCES AND WORSHIP VILLAGE DEITIES...

...WORK IN THE FIELD TRANSPLANTING RICE SAPLINGS...

...AND OFFER PRAYERS AT THE DARGAS OF PIRS*.

* SOURCE: IMPERIAL GAZETTER OF INDIA, 1909

AND BENGALIS WERE A HIGHLY POLITICALLY CONSCIOUS PEOPLE.

RAJA MANSINGH, WHO CARRIED THE MUGHAL STANDARD FROM THE PUNJAB IN THE EAST TO KABUL IN THE WEST, BECAME A HINDU GOVERNOR IN THE HEART OF A MOHAMMEDAN POPULATION.

WHERE IS THE INDIAN GOVERNOR OF A BRITISH PROVINCE? WHERE IS THE INDIAN COMMANDER OF A BRITISH DIVISION? WHERE IS THE INDIAN ADVISER OF A BRITISH VICEROY?

LORD CURZON, THE BRITISH VICEROY, HAD OF COURSE NO INTENTION OF APPOINTING OUR COUNTRYMEN TO HIGH PUBLIC OFFICES.

THE HIGHEST RANKS OF CIVIL EMPLOYMENT IN INDIA MUST BE HELD BY ENGLISHMEN FOR THE REASON THAT...

...THEY POSSESS PARTLY BY HEREDITY, PARTLY BY UPBRINGING, PARTLY BY EDUCATION, THE KNOWLEDGE OF THE PRINCIPLES OF GOVERNMENT, THE HABITS OF MIND, AND THE VIGOUR OF CHARACTER WHICH ARE ESSENTIAL FOR THE TASK.

SURENDRANATH BANERJI — POPULARLY KNOWN AS 'SURRENDER-NOT-BANERJI' THUNDERED —

I PROTEST AGAINST THIS ASSUMPTION OF OUR RACIAL INFERIORITY. ARE INDIANS INFERIOR TO EUROPEANS?

NO! NO! NO!

THE GROWING EXPECTATIONS OF OUR COUNTRYMEN CAUSED DISMAY AMONG BRITISH OFFICIALS.

THE REAL DANGER TO OUR RULE IN INDIA COMES FROM THE EDUCATED INDIANS WHEN THEY ADOPT WESTERN IDEAS OF AGITATION...

BENGALIS! THEY ARE THE CHIEF CULPRITS.

THE BRITISH OFFICIALS REVIVED THE PROPOSAL OF REORGANIZATION OF PROVINCES.

TRANSFER EAST BENGAL TO ASSAM AND FORM A NEW PROVINCE OF EASTERN BENGAL AND ASSAM. MUSLIMS WILL FORM THE MAJORITY IN THE NEW PROVINCE.

AND IN THE OLD PROVINCE BENGALIS WILL BE OUTNUMBERED BY BIHARIS AND ORIYAS.

BENGAL UNITED IS A POWER. BENGAL DIVIDED WILL PULL IN SEVERAL DIRECTIONS.

OUR BENGALI BRETHREN HELD PROTEST MEETINGS. THEY SENT A PETITION SIGNED BY OVER 75,000 PEOPLE TO THE BRITISH PARLIAMENT IN LONDON. THEY TOOK OUT PROCESSIONS.

UNITED BENGAL

UNITY IS STRENGTH

NO PARTITION

BAN MATA

NO PARTITION

BANDE

BUT LORD CURZON REMAINED UNMOVED.

IF WE SHOW OUR WEAKNESS BY YIELDING TO THEIR CLAMOUR WE SHALL NOT BE ABLE TO DIVIDE BENGAL.

BIPIN CHANDRA PAL, ONE OF THE LEADERS, WAS A BITTER MAN.

IF ANYTHING COULD PROVE THE UTTER FUTILITY OF OUR SO-CALLED METHODS OF CONSTITUTIONAL POLITICAL AGITATION... THE HISTORY OF THE AGITATION AGAINST THE PROPOSAL TO PARTITION BENGAL HAS DONE IT.

HOWEVER, POET RABINDRANATH TAGORE REMAINED COOL!

IF A TREE WERE TO PLEAD WITH THE MAN — YOUR BLOWS WILL KILL ME — WOULD IT BE SPARED?

TURN AWAY FROM OLD-STYLE POLITICS, TRYING IN VAIN TO PLACATE THE FOREIGN RULER AND TALKING BIG IN A FOREIGN LANGUAGE. GO TO THE VILLAGES.

TILL THEN THE USUAL PRACTICE WAS TO HOLD MEETINGS IN CALCUTTA AND OTHER TOWNS, SUBMIT PETITIONS IN ENGLISH AND DELIVER TALKS IN ENGLISH.

VOLUNTEERS BEGAN TO MOBILIZE PUBLIC OPINION IN VILLAGES AND SMALL TOWNS.

FIRANGEES ARE A NATION OF MERCHANTS. THEY UNDERSTAND ONE LANGUAGE. BOYCOTT.

BOYCOTT MANCHESTER CLOTH. PRACTISE SWADESHI... WE WILL UNITE DIVIDED BENGAL.

PRAYERS AGAINST PARTITION WERE HELD IN MOSQUES IN MYMENSINGH, BARISAL AND SERAMPORE...

... AND AT KALIGHAT TEMPLE, CALCUTTA —

MOTHER, STANDING BEFORE YOUR HOLY PRESENCE I TAKE A VOW TO BOYCOTT FOREIGN GOODS AND ADHERE TO THE PRINCIPLE OF SWADESHI.

HINDU AND MUSLIM STUDENTS OF CALCUTTA MARCHED HAND IN HAND AND HELD A 10,000-STRONG RALLY WHERE THEIR LEADER, ABDUL RASUL DECLARED —

WE, BOTH HINDUS AND MUSLIMS, BELONG TO THE SAME MOTHER — BENGAL.

BUT CURZON HAD OTHER IDEAS.

THE PARTITION WILL COME INTO EFFECT ON SIXTEENTH OCTOBER.*

AND POET RABINDRANATH SPOKE FOR ALL BENGAL —

WE WILL OBSERVE SIXTEENTH OCTOBER NOT AS PARTITION DAY BUT AS UNITY DAY.

* IN THE YEAR 1905

16TH OCTOBER, 1905. MEN AND WOMEN, RICH AND POOR, HINDUS AND MUSLIMS WALKED BAREFOOT TO THE BANKS OF THE GANGA AND EXCHANGED RAKHIS.

BROTHERS, LET US REMAIN UNITED!

RABINDRANATH TAGORE DASHED INTO THE NAKHODA MASJID ...

... EMBRACED THE MULLAS AND TIED RAKHIS TO THEIR WRISTS.

BROTHERS, LIVE UNITED.

BANDE MATARAM

RAKHIS WERE TIED TO THE POLICEMEN AND EVEN TO THE EUROPEANS.

BROTHERS, LIVE UNITED!

BANDE MATARAM

BANDE MATARAM.

PEOPLE BOYCOTTED FOREIGN GOODS.

NO, SIR. MANCHESTER CLOTH IS NOT FOR ME. SHOW ME SWADESHI CLOTH.

!

MILL CLOTH FROM BOMBAY AND AHMEDABAD COULD NOT MEET THE DEMAND. OUR PEOPLE APPROACHED THE VILLAGE WEAVERS.

WHAT! YOU WANT HANDLOOM CLOTH!

YES TONS AND TONS.

WEAVERS DUSTED THE DISCARDED LOOMS AND SET TO WORK.

THIS MILL YARN IS COARSE! I WISH I'D PRESERVED THE CHARKHA.

CHARKHA WITH WHICH YARN WAS SPUN WAS HARD TO FIND. WEAVERS HAD TO USE MILL-MADE YARN.

THUS MEN AND WOMEN DISCARDED CHEAP AND FINE MANCHESTER CLOTH IN FAVOUR OF COARSE HANDLOOM FABRICS.

YOU SAY IT IS COARSE. I SAY IT IS BEAUTIFUL. IT IS OURS!

GIVE THE PLACE OF HONOUR TO THE COARSE CLOTH, SISTER. THIS IS THE GIFT OF THE MOTHER TOO POOR TO OFFER A BETTER ONE.

THUS THE SWADESHI MOVEMENT REVIVED THE INDIGENOUS HANDLOOM INDUSTRY.

WOMEN REMOVED THEIR BANGLES.

THIS IS THE VILAYATI BANGLE.

PRIESTS REFUSED TO TOUCH SWEETS MADE OF FOREIGN SUGAR.

GOD WILL BE DISPLEASED IF YOU OFFER VILAYATI MATERIAL.

MEN GAVE UP SMOKING.

WHAT TO DO. SWADESHI CIGARETT-ES ARE ALWAYS IN SHORT SUPPLY.

AND THEY REFUSED TO TOUCH FOREIGN LIQUOR.

WOMEN WANTED SWADESHI MATCHES.

YOU'D BETTER GET ME SWADESHI MATCHES. OTHERWISE YOU MAY HAVE TO GO WITHOUT FOOD.

CHILDREN WANTED SWADESHI PAPER, SWADESHI INK AND SWADESHI NIBS.

LISTEN TO ME, CHILD. THESE NIBS BREAK. YOUR HANDWRITING WILL BE SPOILED.

WHAT I WRITE WITH SWADESHI NIB IS THE MOST BEAUTIFUL WRITING.

A CHAIN OF SWADESHI STORES CAME INTO EXISTENCE ALL OVER BENGAL. HOWEVER, SOME UNSCRUPULOUS TRADERS DID NOT HESITATE TO HIKE THE PRICE OF SWADESHI GOODS THAT WERE SCARCE.

YOU HAVE TO PAY MORE IF YOU WANT SWADESHI GOODS.

TO PUT A STOP TO MALPRACTICES SEVERAL SAMITIS WERE FORMED. SCHOOL AND COLLEGE BOYS SOLD GOODS AT COST PRICE.

GOD BLESS YOU, SON. AT LAST I GOT THE SWADESHI GOODS AT A FAIR PRICE.

THE SAMITIS ORGANIZED MEETINGS, TOOK OUT PROCESSIONS, DISTRIBUTED PATRIOTIC LITERATURE.

BANDE MATARAM.

BANDE MATARAM

FULLER, THE LT. GOVERNOR OF THE NEW PROVINCE OF EAST BENGAL, WAS ALARMED.

STUDENTS ARE THE BACKBONE OF THE SWADESHI MOVEMENT. WE MUST PREVENT THEM FROM JOINING IT.

THE HEADMASTERS OF SCHOOLS RECEIVED CIRCULARS FROM THE GOVERNMENT ASKING THEM TO TAKE STRICT ACTION AGAINST OFFENDING STUDENTS.

KALIPRASANNA DASGUPTA, THE HEADMASTER OF MADARIPUR SCHOOL, CALLED A MEETING OF HIS STUDENTS.

THE GOVERNMENT HAS BANNED THE RAISING OF THE SLOGAN— BANDE MATARAM.

I DO NOT KNOW WHAT YOU HAVE TO SAY. AS FAR AS I AM CONCERNED I HAVE ONLY TWO WORDS TO SAY.

BANDE MATARAM.

STUDENTS CHEERED THEIR HEADMASTER AND RESPONDED IN SIMILAR WORDS.

BANDE MATARAM

IT IS NEEDLESS TO SAY THAT DASGUPTA LOST HIS JOB.

AT RANGPUR* 263 BOYS WHO DEFIED THE GOVERNMENT ORDER AND ATTENDED SWADESHI MEETINGS WERE THROWN OUT OF THE SCHOOL.

WE ARE HAPPY WE DON'T HAVE TO ATTEND THE GOVERNMENT SCHOOL.

WE WANT SWADESHI SCHOOLS WHERE PATRIOTISM IS NOT CONSIDERED A CRIME.

RANGPUR HAD THE DISTINCTION OF SETTING UP THE FIRST NATIONAL SCHOOL.

* NOW IN BANGLA DESH

NATIONAL SCHOOLS SPRANG UP IN CITIES, TOWNS AND VILLAGES. AT RAMARA IN FARIDPUR, CLASSES WERE HELD AT THE HOUSE OF A MUSLIM...

COME, CHILDREN, COME.

... AND IN DHALGRAM THE NATIONAL SCHOOL WAS THROWN OPEN TO NAMASHUDRAS.*

IN CALCUTTA TWO INSTITUTIONS CAME INTO BEING — THE NATIONAL COUNCIL OF EDUCATION AND THE SOCIETY FOR THE PROMOTION OF TECHNICAL EDUCATION. THOUSANDS OF STUDENTS BOYCOTTED OFFICIAL EDUCATIONAL INSTITUTIONS AND SOUGHT ADMISSION TO NATIONAL SCHOOLS AND COLLEGES.

OUR COURSE IS NOT RECOGNIZED BY THE GOVERNMENT. YOU WILL NOT GET JOBS IN THE GOVERNMENT.

I HAVE NO INTENTION OF BECOMING A GUMASTA IN A GOVERNMENT OFFICE, SIR.

AND POET RABINDRANATH CONTINUED HIS WORK AT SANTINIKETAN,

* A SECT OF SHUDRAS WHO WERE ELEVATED IN THEIR SOCIAL STATUS BY THEIR LONG ASSOCIATION WITH THE BRAHMANAS.

THE INDIAN NATIONAL CONGRESS MET AT VARANASI IN 1905. SURENDRANATH BANERJI RECEIVED A STANDING OVATION.

BANDE MATARAM.

LORD CURZON HAS SOUGHT TO BRING ABOUT THE DISINTEGRATION OF OUR RACE. HAS HE SUCCEEDED?

NO!

NO!

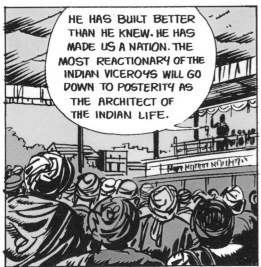

HE HAS BUILT BETTER THAN HE KNEW. HE HAS MADE US A NATION. THE MOST REACTIONARY OF THE INDIAN VICEROYS WILL GO DOWN TO POSTERITY AS THE ARCHITECT OF THE INDIAN LIFE.

YES. THE ENTIRE NATION TOOK UP SWADESHI AND BOYCOTT OF EUROPEAN GOODS.

IN MADRAS WOMEN OPTED FOR SWADESHI FABRICS AND SANG SONGS IN PRAISE OF SWADESHI.

IN PUNJAB, U.P. AND EVEN IN SOME AREAS OF THE SOUTH, *VANDE MATARAM* BECAME A FORM OF GREETING.

VANDE MATARAM.

VANDE MATARAM.

WHEN LORD CURZON WAS SUCCEEDED BY LORD MINTO, OUR BENGALI BRETHREN HOPED THAT THE NEW VICEROY WOULD TAKE NOTE OF POPULAR DISCONTENT AND ANNOUNCE ANNULMENT OF PARTITION. HOWEVER WHEN A DELEGATION CALLED ON HIM —

I AM EXTREMELY SORRY, GENTLEMEN. PARTITION IS A SETTLED FACT. WE CANNOT REOPEN THE QUESTION.

LORD MINTO'S REPLY MADE PEOPLE EVEN MORE FRUSTRATED AND ANGRY. A HUGE FIRE WAS LIT AT COLLEGE SQUARE IN CALCUTTA.

THE ONLOOKERS THREW DOWN INTO THE FIRE CHUDDARS, SALWARS, SHOES, CIGARETTES— ANYTHING MANUFACTURED BY THE BRITISH.

PEOPLE INTENSIFIED THE AGITATION. THE GOAL NOW WAS FREEDOM FROM THE BRITISH RULE AS POINTED OUT BY BIPIN CHANDRA PAL AND AUROBINDO.

OUR IDEAL IS FREEDOM WHICH MEANS ABSENCE OF FOREIGN CONTROL.

THE NEW MOVEMENT IS NOT PRIMARILY A PROTEST AGAINST BAD GOVERNMENT. IT IS A PROTEST AGAINST THE CONTINUANCE OF BRITISH CONTROL, WHETHER THAT CONTROL IS USED WELL OR ILL, JUSTLY OR UNJUSTLY, IS A MINOR AND INESSENTIAL CONSIDERATION.

A LARGE NUMBER OF WORKERS EMPLOYED IN BRITISH FIRMS STRUCK WORK. MUSLIM DRIVERS OF THE EASTERN BENGAL RAILWAY TOOK A PLEDGE ON THE QURAN AND WALKED OUT TO JOIN THE SWADESHI MOVEMENT.

THE BOYCOTT MOVEMENT WAS INTENSIFIED. VOLUNTEERS BEGAN PEACEFUL PICKETING IN FRONT OF SHOPS.

BROTHER, I BEG YOU, DON'T BUY VILAYATI GOODS.

IN CASE THEY SAW SOMEONE COMING OUT OF THE SHOP —

SISTER, HAVE YOU BOUGHT VILAYATI GOODS...

Y...E...S...

IT IS DIFFICULT TO GET SWADESHI...

WE WILL ARRANGE IT FOR YOU. PLEASE RETURN THE GOODS.

IF THE SHOPKEEPER REFUSED TO TAKE BACK THE GOODS SOLD, THE VOLUNTEER WOULD PAY FOR THE GOODS AND CONSIGN THEM TO THE FIRE.

HERE IS THE PAYMENT FOR YOUR....

NO, PLEASE. THIS IS THE LAST TIME I TOUCH VILAYATI GOODS.

SOME YOUNG MEN WOULD GET INTO AN ARGUMENT WITH THOSE WHO WISHED TO BUY FOREIGN GOODS—

YOUR MONEY MUST GO TO OUR POOR WEAVERS, NOT TO THE MANCHESTER BARONS.

PLEASE STAND ASIDE AND LET ME PASS.

IF YOU STILL INSIST ON BUYING VILAYATI GOODS...

YOU COULD WALK ON OUR BODIES.

!

THAT WAS THE SIGNAL FOR THE POLICE TO COME RUSHING...

...WIELDING LATHIS.

BANDE MATARAM

15

CONTD. ON PAGE NO. 18

FULLER, THE LT. GOVERNOR OF THE NEW PROVINCE OF EAST BENGAL, DID NOT HESITATE TO ADOPT RUTHLESS MEASURES TO BREAK THE AGITATION.

YOU WILL SEE TO IT THAT NO ONE RAISES THE CRY BANDE MATARAM.

URCHINS WHO SHOUTED BANDE MATARAM WERE GIVEN A CHASE...

BANDE MATARAM

... CAUGHT ...

BANDE MATARAM

... AND FLOGGED.

BANDE MATARAM

DO YOU SEE WHAT IS WRITTEN ON THE WALL... PULL DOWN THAT HOUSE.

BANDE MATARAM

IN SPITE OF SUCH HARSH MEASURES PEOPLE REFUSED TO BOW DOWN BEFORE FULLER. AT BARISAL —

WE WILL HOLD A PROVINCIAL CONFERENCE ON APRIL 14TH AND 15TH.

ON THE 14TH THE DELEGATES TO THE CONFERENCE TOOK OUT A PROCESSION. BARRISTER ABDUL RASUL WAS TO BE THE PRESIDENT. HE WAS IN A CARRIAGE WITH HIS ENGLISH WIFE. SURENDRANATH AND OTHERS FOLLOWED THE CARRIAGE ON FOOT.

BANDE MATARAM

THE POLICE ALLOWED THE LEADERS TO PASS UNMOLESTED. HOWEVER THEY RAISED THEIR LATHIS AS THE YOUNGER DELEGATES PASSED BY.

BANDE MATARAM

A VOLUNTEER CALLED CHITTARANJAN WAS BODILY THROWN INTO A TANK FILLED WITH WATER...

BANDE MATARAM

... AND LATHI BLOWS WERE SHOWERED ON THE YOUNG MAN STRUGGLING IN THE TANK.

BANDE MATARAM

HEARING THE COMMOTION AT THE BACK SURENDRANATH TURNED BACK.

WHY ARE YOU THRASHING THEM? I AM RESPONSIBLE FOR THEIR BEHAVIOUR. ARREST ME, IF YOU LIKE.

YOU ARE MY PRISONER, SIR.

SURENDRANATH WAS TAKEN PRISONER AND LATER SET FREE. ON HIS WAY BACK TO CALCUTTA HE RECEIVED AN ENTHUSIASTIC WELCOME AT EVERY PLACE. WHEN HE REACHED CALCUTTA IT WAS JUST BEFORE DAY-BREAK. OVER TEN THOUSAND PEOPLE GREETED HIM.

THE EXCITED YOUNGSTERS UNHORSED THE CARRIAGE AND DREW IT TO COLLEGE SQUARE WHERE HE ADDRESSED A MEETING.

THE BARISAL INCIDENT ELECTRIFIED THE NATION. AND LORD MINTO RECEIVED A STRONG NOTE FROM THE GOVERNMENT IN ENGLAND.

WHAT WAS THE CASE? PARTITION WAS UNPOPULAR. HOW COULD YOU PROCURE AN ABATEMENT? CLEARLY BY TRYING TO GIVE AGITATORS AS LITTLE TO CRY OUT ABOUT AS POSSIBLE.

FULLER IS A FOOL.

HOWEVER, THE SITUATION HAD GONE OUT OF CONTROL. LORD MINTO ISSUED AN ORDINANCE RESTRICTING THE RIGHT TO HOLD MEETINGS. BUT THE AGITATORS WERE READY WITH AN ANSWER.

ONLY MEETINGS ARE BANNED. NOT SINGING. NOT FESTIVALS. NOT PLAYS.

THE SPEAKER WAS LIAKAT HUSAIN.

BOYS TRAINED BY LIAKAT HUSAIN, HIMSELF A MELODIOUS SINGER, WENT ROUND SINGING SONGS...

THE TIGHTER THEIR NOOSE, THE EASIER WOULD IT BE TO BREAK // THE EASIER FOR US TO BE FREE // THE MORE THEIR EYES TURN RED, THE MORE OUR EYES WILL OPEN // MORE OPEN WILL OUR EYES BE //

... WHICH THE COMMON FOLK BEGAN TO HUM.

ARE YOU SO STRONG TO SEVER THE CHAIN OF DESTINY? // OH! YOU THINK YOU ARE SO STRONG! // THE PRIDE TO BREAK AND MAKE OUR LIVES AT WILL // OH! TO BE SO PROUD YOU LONG! //

LET THE EARTH AND THE WATER AND THE AIR AND THE FRUITS OF BENGAL BE HOLY, MY LORD! // LET THE LIVES AND THE MINDS OF ALL THE BROTHERS AND SISTERS OF BENGAL BE ONE, MY LORD! //

LET'S ACCEPT WITH REVERENCE, THE COARSE CLOTH THAT OUR MOTHER GIVES US! // SHE IS DRAINED OF HER RICHES, MY BROTHERS // THAT'S ALL SHE CAN AFFORD TO GIVE US //

THE BEAUTY, THE SHADE, THE LOVE, THE TENDERNESS // IN THY LOVING ARMS BECKONING TO US, SPREAD FOR US // UNDER YOUR TREES AND ON THE BANKS OF YOUR RIVERS! //

FOLK TALES AND DRAMAS WERE SUITABLY MODIFIED.

AND HANUMAN SET THE WHOLE LANKA ON FIRE.

TO SERVE OUR MOTHERLAND EACH ONE OF US MUST BECOME A HANUMAN.

BAIRAGIS AND VAISHNAVIS BEGAN TO SING SWADESHI SONGS.

MUKUNDA DAS COMPOSED JATRAS* WITH PATRIOTIC THEMES.

AND FOLK POET MOFIZUDDIN BAYATI COMPOSED SWADESHI SONGS IN THE TRADITIONAL FORM.

AND HISTORICAL PLAYS THAT INSPIRED PATRIOTISM WERE STAGED. THEY INCLUDED SIRAJUDDAULAH, CHHATRAPATI SHIVAJI, DURGADAS, PALASIR PRAYASHCHITTA, SABASH BANGALI, MEWAR PATAN, MIR KASIM AND OTHERS.

SOON GOVERNMENT WOKE UP TO THE REAL PURPOSE OF THESE PLAYS AND SOME OF THESE WERE BANNED.

* A FORM OF FOLK-THEATRE IN WHICH PERFORMERS COMMUNICATE FREELY WITH THE AUDIENCE.

THE COMMON PEASANTS WERE NOT INTERESTED IN THE POLITICS OF PARTITION.

ALL NEW SCHEMES BENEFIT ONLY ONE PERSON— THE ZAMINDAR, BE HE A HINDU OR A MUSLIM.

I AGREE. BUT MUST WE PAY ENHANCED RATES? CAN WE AFFORD IT?

HARE WROTE—

THEY ARE MORE LIKELY TO FIGHT THEIR HINDU LANDLORDS IF SO DIRECTED.

THE ANGER AGAINST ZAMINDARS WAS ALREADY THERE. IT NEEDED ONLY A SPARK TO EXPLODE. AND EXPLODE IT DID. MUSLIM SERVANTS DEFIED THEIR MASTERS—

... AND RIOTS BROKE OUT IN COMILLA, MYMENSINGH AND A COUPLE OF OTHER PLACES.

HOUSES OF ZAMINDARS AND MONEY-LENDERS WERE RANSACKED. GRAIN LOOTED AND PROMISSORY NOTES SET ON FIRE.

IN SEVERAL PLACES PEASANTS HAPPENED TO BE MUSLIMS AND THE LANDLORDS HINDUS. HOWEVER, HINDU PEASANTS ALSO JOINED IN THE PLUNDER, AND MUSLIM PEASANTS DID NOT HESITATE IN LOOTING MUSLIM LANDLORDS.

IT WAS A CASE OF PLUNDER OF THE RICH BY THE POOR.

ON HEARING THE NEWS OF THE RIOTS, LIAKAT HUSAIN RUSHED TO MYMENSINGH.

NO.
WE WILL NOT PERMIT YOU TO TALK TO ANYONE. FIRST WE HAVE TO SEARCH YOU.

THE POLICE FOUND URDU PAMPHLETS.

THESE URGE THE MUSLIMS TO STOP ASSAULTING HINDUS AND INSTEAD UNITE TO FIGHT THE COMMON ENEMY — THE FIRANGEES.

THROW HIM INTO PRISON.

THE BRITISH OFFICIALS WERE HAPPY.

THE RIOTS PROVE ONE THING. MUSLIMS ARE IN FAVOUR OF PARTITION.

SEVERAL NATIONAL LEADERS BLAMED THE GOVERNMENT FOR INCITING THE MUSLIMS.

THEY WANT TO DIVIDE US SO THAT THEY CAN RULE.

TAGORE DECLARED—

THAT THE MUSLIMS COULD BE USED AGAINST THE HINDUS IS A REALLY WORRYING FACT. WHO USED THEM IS NOT IMPORTANT.

A GREAT OCEAN SEPARATED US EDUCATED FEW FROM MILLIONS IN OUR COUNTRY... COME DOWN INTO THE MIDST OF THE PEOPLE... SO THAT HIGH AND LOW, HINDUS AND MUSLIMS AND CHRISTIANS CAN COME TOGETHER, MINGLING HEART WITH HEART, EFFORT WITH EFFORT.

THE BOYCOTT OF EUROPEAN GOODS CONTINUED. THOSE WHO REFUSED TO OBSERVE SWADESHI HAD TO FACE SOCIAL OSTRACIZATION.

NO, BABU. I WON'T WASH VILAYATI CLOTHES.

THIS IS A VILAYATI SHOE, ISN'T IT? SORRY, SIR. I CAN'T TOUCH IT.

I AM SORRY, SIR. I CANNOT GIVE YOU A HAIR CUT. YOU DO NOT WEAR SWADESHI.

AMMA, I HAVE NO FRIENDS. NO ONE WANTS TO PLAY WITH ME. THEY SAY WE USE VILAYATI GOODS. AMMA... PLEASE.

HOW CAN WE CONSIDER A MARRIAGE ALLIANCE WITH YOUR FAMILY? YOU DON'T OBSERVE SWADESHI, DO YOU?

THERE WERE CASES OF POOR PEOPLE SUFFERING ON ACCOUNT OF THE BOYCOTT.

SWADESHI MAAL IS EXPENSIVE. I CANNOT AFFORD IT. YET I HAVE TO BUY IT OUT OF FEAR.

26

MEANWHILE A FEW YOUNG MEN WERE GETTING IMPATIENT. THEY FORMED REVOLUTIONARY GROUPS AND DECIDED TO STRIKE ALTHOUGH THEY KNEW THEY WERE NO MATCH FOR THE BRITISH POWER.

THE FIRST EVER BOMB WAS EXPLODED BY KHUDIRAM BOSE ON APRIL 30, 1908.

MANY REVOLUTIONARIES WERE ROUNDED UP AND AUROBINDO GHOSH WAS ALSO IMPLICATED IN THE CASE. HIS FRIEND C.R. DAS SAID IN THE COURT.

MY APPEAL TO YOU THEREFORE IS THAT A MAN LIKE THIS... STANDS TRIAL NOT ONLY BEFORE THIS BAR, BUT BEFORE THE HIGH COURT OF HISTORY. LONG AFTER THIS CONTROVERSY IS HUSHED... THE WORLD WILL LOOK UPON HIM AS A PROPHET OF NATIONALISM AND A LOVER OF HUMANITY.

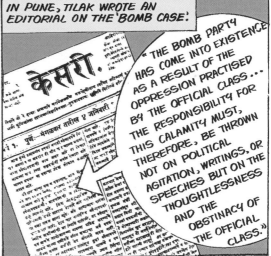

IN PUNE, TILAK WROTE AN EDITORIAL ON THE 'BOMB CASE.'

" THE BOMB PARTY HAS COME INTO EXISTENCE AS A RESULT OF THE OPPRESSION PRACTISED BY THE OFFICIAL CLASS... THE RESPONSIBILITY FOR THIS CALAMITY MUST, THEREFORE, BE THROWN NOT ON POLITICAL AGITATION, WRITINGS, OR SPEECHES BUT ON THE THOUGHTLESSNESS AND THE OBSTINACY OF THE OFFICIAL CLASS. "

THE GOVERNMENT ARRESTED TILAK ON THE CHARGES OF SEDITION.

...FOR ME IT CAN ONLY BE A MATTER OF A FEW YEARS, BUT FUTURE GENERATIONS WILL LOOK TO YOUR VERDICT AND SEE WHETHER YOU HAVE JUDGED WRONG OR RIGHT. THE VERDICT MAY LIKELY BE A MEMORABLE ONE IN THE HISTORY OF THE FREEDOM OF THE INDIAN PRESS...

TILAK WAS SENTENCED TO SIX YEARS' DEPORTATION. ON THE DAY THE JUDGEMENT WAS ANNOUNCED, MILL WORKERS IN BOMBAY DECIDED TO STRIKE WORK. THE STRIKE LASTED FOR SIX DAYS.

MILLS L

TILAK WAS DEPORTED TO MANDALAY. "VANDE MATARAM" WROTE :

GO, TILAK, WHEREVER YOU MAY BE SENT TO CRUSH YOUR BODY... THE CANKER OF THE CHAINS WILL NOT ONLY EAT INTO YOUR LIMBS BUT ALSO INTO EVERY HEART OF THE COUNTRY TO STIR IT UP TO ITS DUTY. YOU HAVE FULFILLED YOUR MISSION...

SIMILARLY NINE REVOLUTIONARIES OF BENGAL WERE DEPORTED. BUT THE REVOLUTIONARIES BETRAYED NO FEAR. WHEN ULLASKAR DUTTA ON TRIAL FOR LIFE BROKE OUT INTO A PATRIOTIC SONG THE WHOLE COURT STOOD UP IN HIS HONOUR.

BLESSED IS MY BIRTH THAT I AM BORN IN THIS LAND. BLESSED IS MY LIFE, FOR I LOVE YOU, O MY MOTHERLAND.

ANOTHER REVOLUTIONARY, HEMACHANDRA LEFT FOR THE ANDAMANS WITH A SMILE ON HIS FACE.

HOWEVER, THE SWADESHI MOVEMENT GRADUALLY LOST ITS VIGOUR. IN JUNE 1909 AUROBINDO STEPPED OUT OF THE PRISON...

... AND PAUSED FOR A WHILE. ONLY SILENCE GREETED HIM.

LATER HE SAID —

WHEN I WENT INTO JAIL THE WHOLE COUNTRY WAS ALIVE WITH THE CRY OF 'BANDE MATARAM'... WHEN I CAME OUT OF JAIL I LISTENED FOR THE CRY BUT THERE WAS INSTEAD, SILENCE.

OF COURSE THE SWADESHI MOVEMENT DID ACHIEVE ITS OBJECTIVE WHEN LORD HARDINGE, THE NEW VICEROY, REVOKED PARTITION ON ASSUMPTION OF OFFICE. THE SPIRIT OF SWADESHI AND BOYCOTT WOULD LATER BE REVIVED BY MAHATMA GANDHI. MEANWHILE POET RABINDRANATH URGED —

MOVE, O TREADERS OF LONG AND DIFFICULT PATH, MOVE BY DAY AND MOVE BY NIGHT — CARRY ON WITH YOUR VICTORY-MARCH.

The Swadeshi Enterprise

The discovery of the steam engine which could haul railway carriages and run textile looms, marked the beginning of the Industrial Revolution in Europe in the eighteenth century. The British killed indigenous industry in India so that their manufacturers could find a ready market in our country. And they tried their best to keep India industrially backward and dependent on European countries for its requirements. However, in spite of their best efforts to keep India off the map of the industrial world, an industrial revolution, on a much smaller scale no doubt, did take place in 1905. If it was the power of steam that launched the Industrial Revolution in Europe, it was the power of swadeshi which launched it in India.

Long before the swadeshi movement was launched, our leaders like Romesh Chandra Dutt had been advocating swadeshi enterprise. Kishorilal Mukherji started the Sibpur Iron Works in 1867, and in the same year, a Hindu Mela was held in Calcutta to exhibit and sell swadeshi crafts. In 1893 Prafulla Chandra Ray started his company, Bengal Chemicals. Later, he said, "Our educated young men, the moment they came out of their colleges were on the look-out for a situation or a soft job under the Government, or failing that, in a European mercantile firm. The professions were becoming overcrowded. A few came out of the engineering college, but they too were helpless seekers after jobs. . . . What to do with all these young men? How to bring bread to the mouths of the ill-fed, famished young men of the middle classes?"

Prafulla Chandra Ray made a beginning by providing jobs for educated youth when he launched Bengal Chemicals. And a few mills which produced cotton yarn were functioning in Ahmedabad and Bombay long before 1905.

The swadeshi movement came as a shot in the arm for swadeshi enterprise. Our countrymen were convinced that they should patronise swadeshi goods in preference to foreign goods, even if they were more expensive and of inferior quality. With the boycott of foreign goods, there was a spurt in the demand for swadeshi goods, and men with ideas, money and enthusiasm, rose to the occasion. A chain of swadeshi emporiums started marketing swadeshi goods. There was a great demand for the mill yarn of Bombay and Ahmedabad. Brass and bell-metal utensils edged out those made of imported enamelled metals.

In the war of nibs, swadeshi nibs emerged victorious. Swadeshi teacups, saucers, tea-pots, inkpots and dolls, not only captured the hearts and purses of our countrymen, they also entered the foreign market! When the mind was full of swadeshi thoughts, could the body be cleansed with foreign soap? No. So foreign toilet soaps hastily made way for swadeshi soap. And sacred fires in sanctum sanctorums and the fires in kitchens came to be lit with swadeshi matchsticks. Even smokers chose to 'burn' swadeshi cigarettes! Paper, candles, sugar, bicycles began to be manufactured in our country *without* any support from the foreign government. Our entrepreneurs also entered the field of banking and insurance.

government, all combined to bring pressure on swadeshi enterprise. Many of these enterprises died. A few survived. Despite heavy odds, new indigenous companies did surface. One such was the Tata Iron & Steel Company in Jamshedpur.

On the political front, the swadeshi movement proved that Indians could fight injustice. On the economic front, it was proved beyond the shadow of a doubt that Indian scientists, engineers, technologists

But the well-entrenched European companies put up a stiff fight. When Mohamed Kalamian launched the Bengal Steam Navigation Company in 1905, European navigation companies drastically reduced the rate for passengers. Jute mills owned by Europeans refused to buy cargo carried by swadeshi ships! Lack of technical know-how, lack of sufficient capital, stiff and unscrupulous competition from European companies and the apathy of the

and workers were in no way inferior to their counterparts in Europe and America. Yet India remained industrially backward because the British rulers saw to it that it remained so. Our entrepreneurs realized that business and industry could not flourish unless the country became independent. What independence means to industrial growth and prosperity can be judged if we compare the state of our industry under British rule with the progress it has made since independence.

Vivekananda taught Self-Esteem

Swami Vivekananda played a significant role in shaking his countrymen out of their deep slumber and inspired them with the ideals of freedom and liberty. In his whirlwind tour of the country from Kanya Kumari to Kashmir, he took the country by storm and his countrymen responded to his call— ARISE! AWAKE! STOP NOT TILL THE GOAL IS REACHED. Although he attained samadhi in 1902, his words continued to inspire his countrymen and the courage he instilled in their hearts found expression during the swadeshi movement.

Excerpts from Swami Vivekananda's writings:

A cloud of impenetrable darkness has at present equally enveloped us all. Now there is neither firmness of purpose nor boldness of enterprise, neither courage of heart, nor strength of mind, neither aversion to maltreatment by others, nor dislike for slavery, neither love in the heart, nor hope, nor manliness; but what we have in India are only deep-rooted envy and strong antipathy against one another, morbid desire to ruin by hook or by crook the weak, and dog-like to lick the feet of the strong. Now the highest satisfaction consists in the display of wealth and power, devotion of self-gratification, wisdom in the accumulation of transitory objects; yoga, in hideous diabolical practices; work, in the slavery of others; civilisation, in base imitation of foreign nations; eloquence, in the use of abusive language; the merit of literature, in extravagant flatteries of the rich or in the diffusion of ghastly obscenities!

... When I see Indians dressed in European apparel and costumes, the thought comes to my mind, perhaps they feel ashamed to own their nationality and kinship with the ignorant, poor, illiterate, downtrodden people of India!

... India! With this mere echoing of others, with this base imitation of others, with this dependence on others, this slavish weakness, this vile detestable cruelty—wouldst thou, with these provisions only, scale the highest pinnacle of civilisation and greatness?... wouldst thou attain, by means of thy disgraceful cowardice, that freedom deserved only by the brave and the heroic? O India! Forget not...

...that the lower classes, the ignorant, the poor, the illiterate, the cobbler, the sweeper, are thy flesh and blood, thy brothers. Thou brave one, be bold, take courage, be proud that thou art an Indian, and proudly proclaim: "I am an Indian, every Indian is my brother." Thou, too, clad with but a rag round thy loins, proudly proclaim at the top of thy voice: "The Indian is my brother, the Indian is my life, India's gods and goddesses are my God. India's society is the cradle of my infancy, pleasure garden of my youth, the sacred heaven, the Varanasi of my old age." Say, brother: "The soil of India is my highest heaven, the good of India is my good," and repeat and pray day and night, "O Thou Lord of Gauri, O Thou Mother of Strength, take away my weakness, take away my unmanliness, and make me a Man!"